379-6
65

Var: V.

WHY JOHNNY CAN'T

RUN, SWIM, PULL,
DIG, SLITHER,
Etc.

Being a Fairytale for the Young at Mind

By

Jason Alexander

SITNALTA PRESS SAN FRANCISCO

WHY JOHNNY CAN'T . . .

Edited by Deirdre J. G. Porter

This book is an underground softcover edition addressed to the new intellectuals:

(1) in recognition of their existence;
(2) for ammunition; and,
(3) for the further purpose of laying the foundation for broader publication.

All the characters in this book are fictitious and any resemblance to actual persons living or dead is largely coincidental.

813.54
A 376 w
1978

Library of Congress Catalogue Card No. 78-58309
International Standard Book Number 0-931826-00-4

SITNALTA PRESS
1881 Sutter Street, #103
San Francisco, California 94115

Made in the United States of America

To the Three A's

TABLE OF CONTENTS

Part the First

THINGS ARE . . .

Chapter I

IN THE BEGINNING

ONCE UPON A TIME, began the old turtle, the world was a most peculiar place. It was run by humans who were a most peculiar kind of animal.

The turtle was the last of a long line of storytellers. This particular turtle was very sincere and careful in his efforts because somehow he knew that *he* was among the last of the storytellers . . . why, he could not say. It was not just because he was one of the few turtle narrators left, nor, on a cultural level, that the long-lived turtles generally had not experienced as many generations and evolutionary changes as their brother animals.

Perhaps, thought the turtle, this telling to this generation of my children shall be the last simply because of age. In that case, he thought, I must take particular care to be accurate and thorough. I must remember everything, he thought, and his thoughts wandered to his many journey-searches when he had told and re-

told the story to himself. He was confident that he could once more narrate his story and perhaps . . . this time. . . .

He awoke from his reveries as he became aware that the many turtle children were getting restive.

The humans were our ancestors, he resumed, and at the beginning of our age everyone agreed they had made a terrible muddle of things. They had become overcivilized. They polluted their cities, spent vast sums on war and preparing for war, and did not sufficiently care for their brother creature.

A
Most
Peculiar
Place

At this time a great disquiet pervaded the people. Everywhere they turned there were negatives, and the positives held forth by various groups seemed to hold no answers, at least for anybody but the proposers. That is until somebody proposed that nothing should be proposed; that there should be an end to growth, to constant change. It was explained that man had lost contact with nature. The answer, it was generally held, was to return to nature.

The return to nature was a two-fold effort, on the one hand by young men and women who lived in

13

communes and grew and made everything themselves and on the other hand by ecologists and scientists who were very educated men and explained that man was wrong to endanger species such as pupfish and liverwort plants or to use saccharine or aerosols.

The species to which man belonged was called Homo sapiens, which, I am told, means man—the thinking animal. Well, to shorten the tale, said the turtle, the upshot was that the people's planners decided

The State Institute of Science and Planning

that it was the mind, the thinking side of man, that had led him away from oneness with nature.

There began a campaign to become more in tune with nature, to emphasize the physical side of man rather than the mental side. Great emphasis was placed on natural foods and natural methods of health. Jogging, massage, and organic vegetables were held in great esteem. The people who practiced the natural philosophy not only regarded themselves as superior beings, but were regarded by others with both interest and envy.

Soon everybody wished he could have the peace of mind of the back-to-earthers. Parents reconciled themselves to being locked into their lives, but sought the best for their children. They provided them with the most progressive of educations, but the world was so poorly ordered that the harder they tried the worse things became. Their children and their children's children tried every innovative technique anyone could think of. Things only grew worse. Yet, somehow, atavistically, everyone knew education was the key; and, finally, came the big break-through. The State Institute of Science and Planning determined that the problem was that man still looked to the mind to solve his problems. This was a fundamental error. The solution: change the emphasis from sapiens to homo. The proof: thinking had always been ineffective; witness the failure of education as then practiced. Henceforth homo (they would no longer call him man) would exist, as befit his species, as a higher animal, and education would proceed on that basis.

Early Homos

As a result, great progress was made; children became much less troublesome. Seldom was heard the question, Why? Soon education was able to do away altogether with questions on the elementary level. Primary education was entirely devoted to development of feelings, and the greatest of these were held to be feelings of identity with the species.

After several generations the World Planning Authority announced a major milestone: homo had developed an instinct of survival. His feelings had become so primary and so ingrained as to constitute an instinct.

A great holiday was declared. Homo no longer needed to think. He now had a genuine instinct. Now real progress could be made, and indeed it was. Within the space of one or two generations homos began to not only think like animals; they started to look like animals.

The sly homos developed pointed ears and noses like the fox. Others became strong, as an ox. The flighty types began to eat less and less. They only pecked at their food. Oxenhomos criticized them for their eating habits since such sorry creatures, though slight, couldn't even pull their own weight.

The flighty types had the last laugh, however, when they began to grow feathers. Their nimbleness easily allowed them to escape the abuse of the oxenhomos. However, they appeared frivolous and spent most of their time feeding on insects. Having very little to offer homoskind, they provoked a great debate amongst its various representatives. Eventually they

Homo Family Celebrating the Declaration of Instinct

were accepted on the grounds of efficiency when even
the oxenhomos, dumb as they were, came to understand that the birdhomos had achieved flight.

The homos kingdom thus became a peculiar mix of
diverse creatures. Some had the head and shoulders of
a bull and some had the head of a bird. Others had the
bodily characteristics of the animals they most favored.
The owlhomos had charge of secondary education and
their constant Who-ing called attention to the disparate
development of homos. Too chaotic, it was said. To
bring order out of chaos, it was decided amongst the
elite of the higher educators that it would be desirable

to create an age of specialization wherein each creature maximized his particular strength and developed it to the fullest. It was decided to appoint representatives to coordinate planning.

Then came a time of great danger to the land. Every group maintained one of its subspecies should be coordinator. When continued disagreement threatened the very continuation of society, they decided to form a collective. Most of the homos really tried to make government by collective work, and it would have except for the sly and the strong.

The oxen and elephant homos, in league with the fox and serpent homos, managed to force or trick all other species out of the Collective Council. That led to a long period of development when first one, then the other, would gain ascendency. During this time, gradual improvement in animalification was made. As each subspecies concentrated on its specialty, the creatures became more and more animal-like.

This was not a bad time in our history, said the turtle, except for two things. It was a time when everybody was too busy to be happy or sad. There was work to do, each according to his kind. It would last from sun-up to sun-down except for the nocturnal creatures (whom the rest suspected of being slothful). Indeed, happiness and sadness weren't really felt anymore amongst the lower animals; it was more a matter of pleasure and pain. If pleasure was rare, well, then in this well-ordered time, so was pain. Who could ask for more? said the Collective Council; that seemed all right to the lower homos.

Other Early Transitional Creatures

It was, rather, in the second area that the trouble began. No matter what their parentage, all creature children were born humanoid. At first this bothered no one since it was no departure from that which had been. Much of the early history of the homos kingdom had been devoted to the education and transformation of humanoid babies into their parental animal types. This was accomplished earlier and earlier with each generation, as a result of a combination of education and training.

Some of the more promising students mutated into hybrid forms as a result of their devotion to their teachers. Universal Education, which had been universally practiced, was made mandatory. In some cases the parents could not recognize their children, particularly after higher education. They were held fortunate by those parents who could recognize their mutated children.

Of course there was no such problem with the subsequent children of mutated parents. Indeed the opposite held true: the more bizarre the offspring became, the more proud the parent.

Homo Vulgaris Mutations
(Retarded)

Homo
Vulgaris
Mutations
(Advanced)

22

*View of Mount Olympus
As Seen Through the Eyes of Mutant Homo*

Then it was that, amongst those of a certain stratum of the homos kingdom, there was discerned the goal thereafter called The Ultimate. The Ultimate, it was whispered, was the subject of a great battle in the last Council of the Collective. Both the sly and the strong wanted to claim The Ultimate as their province of work. This was important because of the very essence of The Ultimate.

The Rule of The Ultimate, as you know, is: From each according to his capacity; to each according to his requirements.

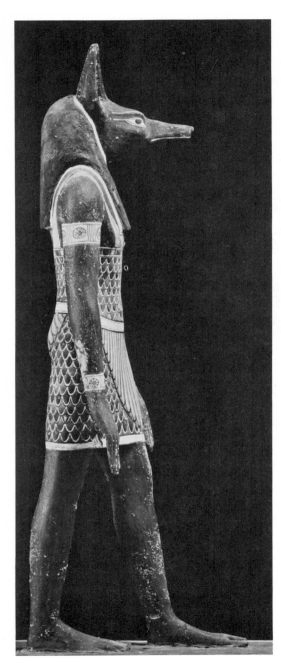

Early
Snox

It was recognized among the higher educated mutants that, as originators of that rule, they were a breed apart from either the higher animals or the lower animals. Among themselves there was no disagreement on this point.

Among themselves, however, there was considerable disagreement on who was more equal, the sly or the strong. The snake-fox clique, called snoxes, claimed their right to serve as administrators or arbiters of The Ultimate, since they had come up with it.

This upset the elephant-oxen clique (who were much given to upset) because they said, No, you didn't, and besides you puny snoxes couldn't enforce any rule even if you wanted to.

Oh, yes we did, said the snoxes nervously (because of the glowering eleoxen). It was revealed to us by the wind which we can hear and it came from an awesome, powerful being who is more powerful than any eleoxen, said one.

Than all eleoxen, said another.

This threw the eleoxen into great discomposure. Can you hear the wind? they asked one another. No, they all replied, but that didn't give them any comfort since all knew snoxes were more discerning than eleoxen. The eleoxen, as was their wont when confused, put up a bully front, stating, We don't believe you heard The Ultimate on the wind. (They didn't deny things could be heard on the wind because any bully knows that somewhere there is someone bigger or tougher than he and lives in terror that around the next corner he might find him.)

Snox Descending a Staircase Bearing The Ultimate

Since snoxes are cowards (but audacious) they said, Look, let's compromise. We will listen to the wind and judge on the application of The Ultimate and you will enforce The Ultimate. Your duty is the most important as you point out, so you shall be kings and we shall be your ministers and become priests. How does that sound to you?

The eleoxen huddled and said, What does the wind say?

The snoxes huddled and said, The wind says, The eleoxen shall be Kings and rule forever and the snoxes shall be my prophets.

How wise is the wind, said the eleoxen. Henceforth the Council of the Collective shall go out of existence and there shall be in its stead the Animal Kingdom which shall be composed of the lower animals, the higher animals, and the ultimate animals.

In acquiescence therewith (support thereof) the snoxes prepared a proclamation establishing the new order. All animals shall live to serve The Ultimate. Interbreeding between the ultimate animals and other animals shall be prohibited. All shall have that schooling or training appropriate to their birth. Animals of burden shall become stronger; animals of production or utility shall produce more or work harder; subterranean animals shall develop greater ability to dig and tunnel; non-terrestrial animals of the air and sea shall fly and swim better. Lower animals and higher animals may only intermarry with permission of the King's Counselors. Neither the royal nor the counselor families may intermarry.

27

And thus the world evolved so as to constitute total justice and eternal harmony except. . . .

Except for the one problem unresolved by the snoxes and eleoxen: The children of the various species were still born humanoid. Why was this critical?

Because of Johnny Eagle.

Chapter II

JOHNNY EAGLE: THE FLEDGLING

JOHNNY EAGLE WAS BORN small and frail as were more and more children of his time.

Such were the problems of the day that few noticed the general shortening of life expectancy and increase in infant mortality. Those who did explained it away as the price society had to pay for progress toward The Ultimate. If some of the species developed the proficiencies (and experienced the consequences) of the shorter-lived animals—well, that was compensated for by their increased fecundity. Their contribution was felt to be the equal of their fellows because in the long run they would commit more generations to the betterment of homoskind. As to infant mortality, well, that was apparent: until the various species could give birth to young of their type it was to be expected that the old-fashioned, out-of-date humanoid babies would largely fail to adjust and prosper in the world into which they were born.

Early Attempts to Develop An Animal Homo . . .

Society, or the Animal Kingdom, or the Civilization of The Ultimate as the snoxes and eleoxen liked to call it, had long known that the secret of infant mortality, and indeed society itself, lay in the early education of its children. As a result of this the snoxes and eleoxen put into effect a program designed to produce good and effective citizens by removing all children from the third day after birth to the Natal Early Start Training centers (snoxes always had a propensity for acronyms). The program was enforced by establishing the duty of every parent to register his offspring for universal conscription within three days after birth. This had been changed from birth because too much paper work was caused by the frequent deaths of the babies within the first three days.

Tom Eagle, Johnny's father, anxious about his child, omitted to register on the third day because he was in constant attendance on his wife, Quen, and his first-born, Johnny. Naturally the organization of society was such that this omission was immediately called to the attention of the eleoxen. While the snoxes had not been able to design a system to effectively reorder rations of milk at training centers, they had devised the most effective of registration systems. This was natural considering priorities, and in consequence

. . . Ultimately Yielded the More Efficient Homo Animal

thereof the Snox Foundation, a think tank, being non-profit, was granted exemption from taxation.

Possibly because Tom had once wondered aloud why those who produced should pay while those who produced nothing should be exempt, he had incurred the wrath of the snoxes. In any case, whether it was the system, the wrath of the snoxes, or simply one of the ubiquitous patriotic informers, on the fourth day Tom was removed from Quen's bedside to the government interrogation center for an inquiry (less formal than inquisition procedures) into his failure to register a birth.

The magistrate dismissed the inquiry upon being informed that the subject child was likely to die shortly. After all, it was clear that the state owed no obligation to its citizens, such as training their children, when such training wouldn't result in a contribution to society.

Tom had said nothing in his defense. In fact, Tom said nothing. Tom was somewhat at a loss. He had always held himself to be a loyal citizen. Neither he nor Quen considered themselves out-of-the-ordinary (although they were considered odd by the few who knew them, as in fact they were since those who knew them were few). In a time when life centered around the subspecies organization Tom and Quen were regarded as loners which was both descriptive and an indictment. The Eagle tribe was not surprised at the inquiry into Tom's behavior or, for that matter, at the frailty of his offspring since Tom never held promise of being a contributor to society or even to the clan.

An early species coordinator during Tom's childhood had characterized Tom as destined to be one of society's free-riders. During that more tolerant time it was thought to be a mark of the homoistic side of government that such types were tolerated. Since individuals such as Tom neither drew upon nor had access to the munificence of a benevolent society they had to fend for themselves. Those individuals who couldn't either died or were welcomed back into the fold. Those who did were ignored (except at tax time).

Tom and Quen characteristically focussed their attention personally on their infant Johnny. In a time of want they lavished the only thing of substance they had to give, their love, upon that fragile newborn life they had brought into the world.

Johnny seemed to gather strength from their tender loving care and attention. When he survived the first two weeks Tom and Quen looked at each other, smiled weary smiles, and began to consider the future. Johnny had begun to breathe regularly; his muscle tone was better; and he slept more definitely and awoke more decisively. In the next couple of weeks Quen was to report when Tom returned that Johnny had seemed momentarily to look at her and to react positively to comforts and negatively to pain and denial.

Tom in turn reported on his tour of Natal Early Start Training centers. We are doing everything wrong, he said. The scientifically raised babies are either blindfolded or kept in the dark for the first two weeks. They are never handled by the same homo

A Plethora of (Transitional) Snoxes

twice. If they cry they are not comforted. If they don't, they are provoked.

Together they regarded Johnny. They saw him struggling to focus his eyes on various objects. They saw him react to his world with cries or chortles. In the next weeks they saw him expand his world by extending his perceptions and applications of acquired skills. When Johnny focussed on them and gave his first smile of recognition Tom and Quen came to understand that they were different. Johnny was different. How? Why now?

Those questions, Tom later explained on a visit from Quen, were his personal renascence and gave birth to a freedom no chains could contain. At the time, however, he only felt that he had observed something important. So did Quen and they talked about it. Laboriously they considered and discarded all aspects of Johnny's smile of recognition until they isolated what was singular about this smile: it was at the root an act of cognition. Johnny was thinking.

Of course, exclaimed Quen. He has been all along. Every day was a step beyond the day before. What a chaos must be the world to a newborn infant. What a masterful, powerful thing to bring order out of that chaos.

Suddenly Tom understood why babies were blindfolded or kept in the dark: it was not to mimic animal births. Now he understood why babies were not to see the same face twice: not to keep them from forming attachments, but to keep them from forming order. Now he understood why they were provoked to

cry: not to toughen them for survival, but to teach them that the world is a malevolent place where only the fittest could survive.

As though he had shed his own blindfold Tom saw that the secret of animalification was one's perception of the world as a hostile, oppressive, evil place rather than a place which could be understood, controlled and remade by one to one's comfort and satisfaction. The former was the world of the creature homo and the latter of the creature sapiens.

This awakening, this emergence from chaos, was to be the beginning of the end for Tom Eagle for it had profound effects. The least of these effects was the apparent reversal of his own animalification. He had never progressed as far toward eaglality as most of his peer group. His partially developed physical characteristics had made him the object

Homohetero . . .

of derision from the advanced and of pity from the charitable majority, but his retrogression caused even the latter to look upon him with distaste.

Johnny, meanwhile, had seemed to pass one milestone of maturity and achievement after another. He grew in an orderly progression both tangibly and intangibly.

Tom and Quen were very proud but also very concerned, for while each month Johnny was physically much ahead of where he was the month before, he was also much behind fellow creatures born at the same time. Against creatures his age he was remarkably frail. Partially for this reason, partially by reason of his still-humanoid form, and partially for selfish reasons Tom and Quen kept him out of school. They kept him out of nest school, nursery school, and pre-pre-day school.

. . . *Genesis*

That didn't mean Tom disapproved of schooling or education. To the contrary, at Johnny's first birthday he set out upon a study of schools as he had once set out to study child rearing. What he found apalled him. After discussing the matter he and Quen decided to conduct their own school—a school for one.

Johnny was bright-eyed and eager. He had progressed from hands and knees to walking with one hand; to walking alone; to seldom falling; to stairs; to skipping. In every other aspect save one he progressed in a parallel fashion. It was fascinating to Tom and Quen, now that they knew what was happening, to watch Johnny expand his horizons, his areas of competence and efficacy. The only worrisome thing was that Johnny didn't talk. He laughed and made incidental noises, but he didn't talk—at least not verbally. It worried Tom but Quen kept assuring him Johnny would when he was ready. If he didn't talk with his mouth he did with his eyes. They were forever on the move, lit with wonder, mirth, mischief, questions, or love. Johnny was by turns active and pensive. He seemed to take life head-on, never backing away, just occasionally pausing to sort out and fit in a new experience or, increasingly, a new thought. One could almost see it happen.

Tom, in his quest for learning or, more precisely, learning about learning, had to study not only what can be known but how to know what can be known. It was early apparent that the rejected black and white linear method of learning called books held promise. Tom began to acquire the simplest of them and they became the foundation of what Quen fondly called Tom's School.

School was Johnny's favorite time. He would sit in Tom's lap and look at the picture books or be read a story. He soon liked to point out the things named or to point to the successive words as they were read.

To stay one jump ahead of the voracious Johnny, Tom and Quen had to teach themselves first. While Johnny continued during his second year to develop both physically and mentally, Tom continued his study of education not only for Johnny but for himself. He began a tour of the post-nest schools. He enjoyed immensely meeting the isolated teacher who seemed also to care about learning, with whom he could, as he described it, talk sense.

What particularly discouraged him were his conversations with the educational establishment. Tom could handle teachers being called facilitators; and he tried to grasp the rationale behind open classrooms, differentiated staffing, and behaviour modification. He certainly had no quarrel with the sound of "educating the whole child." If he couldn't make sense of all the new ideas, new philosophies, new techniques and new teaching methods, well, perhaps that just showed he was in fact a layman dealing with professionals or perhaps, as he knew, that he wasn't very well educated himself.

But it appeared to Tom that nothing worked; it looked as if the children being taught were bored, ignorant, and frustrated. It appeared to him that if there were any good ideas they were incompetently imple-

Mother Superior, Natal Early Start Training Centers

mented by incompletely trained facilitators. If any programs were acknowledged bad, once implemented
they were seldom dropped. Students took potluck in
selection of facilitators and methods, not only from
place to place but within one school. And it was
difficult for Tom to understand why facilitators of the
various ages didn't communicate with facilitators of
preceding ages.

On the other hand it wasn't so difficult for him to
understand why the autonomous schools with their
participatory democracy brought near chaos. The neat
programs and field trips to fun places coupled with
distractions in unstructured classes made, as he saw it,
anarchists, not students. It was easy to see why
facilitators' aides were necessary when there were no
goals, no objectives, no purposes, no standards, only
generalities.

What was virtually impossible for him to handle
was the constant emphasis on the students' right to
enjoy life, to be happy. The educators all assured him
that the sole aim of experimentation with the children
was to see that they were well-adjusted. Every student
should love and be loved.

To enjoy life, to be happy, to be well-adjusted and
loved were surely not to be quarrelled with, but, as he
observed to Quen, those words didn't seem to mean
what he meant. If I'm not crazy, Tom told her, then
the snoxes, eleoxen and the facilitators and their aides
have stolen the words.

And thus it was that Tom, having formed certain
judgments about the nature of a proper school, turned

his attention to the nature of words. Why didn't he mean what they meant?

With the exception of Tom's rare forays in search of answers, he, Quen and Johnny largely withdrew from the society of not only their species but all homos as Tom increasingly asked, Why? He didn't come to understand until too late that the only answers he got were those he worked out himself. With that naivete born of the goodwill of the innocent he continually hoped or expected that somebody would have the answers. Without admitting it he would have settled for another somebody who asked questions. Unfortunately he was denied even

that for, while his wife and son subsequently came to have both questions and answers, Tom did not live to see it.

In his third year Johnny had learned to feed himself, to dress himself, and to wash and dry his hands and brush his teeth. And, as Quen had predicted, Johnny talked when he needed to. One day Tom was

Ordinary Nest Homo

absentmindedly rereading a book to Johnny when Johnny corrected Tom's reading of a word. Thereafter Johnny read to Tom or Quen or to himself. It subsequently became a toss-up whether he liked playing with numbers or reading better.

It was toward the end of Johnny Eagle's third year that the tribal spokespersons (formerly species coor-

43

dinators and formerly formerly clan leaders) came to arrest Tom Eagle for the disgrace he had brought upon his tribe. He had, they informed him, asked the question, "Why?" once too often. Whatever possessed him to approach the Snox Chief and the Chief Eleoxen and ask, "Why should one homo live for another?"

What disgrace he had brought upon the tribe! This was the greatest crisis for the Eagle tribe since the last Council of the Collective when the snox-eleoxen clique had punished their ancestors for the sin of pride.

The Eagle tribe had been infamous for its characteristic pride and notorious for its characteristic fierceness. Only the latter survived the last Council of the Collective for the snoxes had shown the prideful eagles to be capricious, advocating compromise in the name of reasonableness but practicing pridefulness.

The eagles are on the horns of a dilemma, the snoxes had said. Admittedly compromise is fundamental to fairness, indeed to society, but their inflexible pride is contradictory. Their base nature causes them to preach one thing and practice another.

They should practice what they preach, the eleoxen had ruled, and the snox-eleoxen clique had threatened to excommunicate the eagle species.

Fortunately, the then species coordinators had been overthrown by the ancestors of the tribal spokespersons who made it their calling to expunge pride from the eagle tribe. Whenever it surfaced, as it did with Tom Eagle, the spokespersons acted quickly and ruthlessly. Those few of the tribe who sought to excuse Tom's transgressions on the grounds that he was not

WILD (FREE)

EARLY

UPSTART

ESTABLISHED

DOGMATIC

MIDEVIL

INHERITOR

CADET

CARRIER

Eagle Tribe Development

45

properly or totally an eagle (witness his physical regression from animalification) were peremptorily overruled by the vindictive spokespersons.

Johnny and Tom had been down by the stream having a picnic lunch and reading to themselves when the spokespersons' constables seized Tom and dragged him away. The bewildered Johnny was flung aside and ignored. His last sight of his father free was Tom's motioning him to be quiet and be still. When they were out of sight, Johnny ran home crying, Mother! Mother! They have arrested Father!

Chapter III

JOHNNY EAGLE: THE YOUTH

THE ARREST WAS THE LAST TIME but one for Johnny Eagle to see his father alive for while Tom welcomed visits from Quen during his incarceration he forbade her to bring Johnny. At first Quen couldn't find Tom or even learn whether he was alive or dead. When she finally located him she found him chained to a wall of an abandoned rock quarry that had been converted into an insane asylum.

The asylum housed society's untrainables. Generally these creatures, mentally defective at or from birth, by reason of such incapacity failed to yield to animalification. Indeed most failed to mature at all since bodily they simply grew up resembling nothing so much as overgrown babies. These latter occupied the highest levels of the quarry and were the recipients of most of the available sunshine and most of the visitors. (It was considered instructive to bring school children around to learn the effects of not learning.)

*Level One Inmate
Visited by Parents*

The next or middle level was inhabited by two other groups: those who in fact did not learn animalification (from functional, not pathologic, causes) and those who had learned but found they couldn't cope.

Tom was located in the third or lowest level which was almost never used. It was reserved for the remaining category: creatures without mental defect, who had learned, who could cope, but who were obviously crazy.

Tom was obviously crazy. At his commitment hearing (not public) both his behavior and appearance counted against him. As to behavior, surely no one but a madman would question the most fundamental of society's beliefs. And as to appearance, well, just compare him to the other inmates: it was self evident.

Occasionally some inmates, for disciplinary reasons, were cast into the lowest level, the pit. Few survived the dank confines long—those, a month at most. When Quen finally located Tom he had been there six months. She wisely refrained from commiserating. Their reunion in word and deed was devoted to pro-life experience. She brought news from the outside which, being pro-life, was largely about Johnny. Tom absolutely forbade her to bring Johnny, not that his heart didn't ache to see him but rather so that Johnny wouldn't see his father in those circumstances.

Quen visited as often as allowed in the next six months, but that was infrequent. Although Quen called regularly at the asylum her visits were subject to the whim of the Head Keeper. Tom, however, had more frequent visits after the first year for even in his incarceration he had attracted a certain degree of notoriety.

When society's reeducators had visited the asylum to save level two inmates they had heard of Tom. When they found him still alive on subsequent visits, contrary to all expectations since Tom had not only suffered the physical rigors of the pit but the mental one of being alone (the ultimate penalty), they decided to look at him. Being snox faction creatures they could (and did) ask, Why? Tom struck a deal. He would tell them why if Quen could listen. Why not, they agreed; what harm can come of it? He thinks he's fooling us, but it's only a base plea for a selfish purpose.

And thus it came to pass that Quen saw more of Tom in the second year.

Johnny had continued to grow physically stronger and more agile. He had continued his education as well, both because his father would have liked it so and because he liked it so himself. The challenge and rigors of numbers brought concentrated occupation to the boy and eased the loneliness he felt.

Tom, who had time to think, thought a great deal about Johnny. Tell him he must continue his studies, he told Quen. Feed and nurture his curiosity, his de-

sire to understand. I am convinced from my tour of schools that it is important to establish early a way of approaching life. If he has an active mind and confronts life as a challenge he will have the richest patrimony I can provide. In later years Quen would blink back the tears as she considered the consequences of Tom's bequest.

It was in Johnny's fifth year that the reeducators began to work in earnest on Tom Eagle. First he was asked the secret of his survival.

I think it's because I think, he told them (and Quen).

What, they wanted to know, did he think about?

Words, Tom replied.

Some of Society's Reeducators

Why?

Because they are important. They are the basis for everything we do. How can anything that important be so ill-understood? What is understanding? *What* is understood? How do we understand? When and if we do, or don't, so what? These are the things I think about, he told them.

They were very unhappy. They wanted answers, not questions. Tom was threatened with torture if he didn't tell his secret of resistance to death. Tom told them they were welcome to anything he knew without torture.

Why? What was the trick?

Tom had no answer to that either.

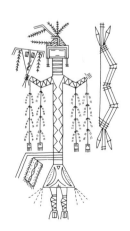

The reeducators considered Tom a challenge. They had him moved up to the middle level, both for greater access and to end his solitary thinking. He was buffeted between two groups of reeducators. On the one hand one group sought to determine and modify Tom's behavior by subjecting him to countless experiments and measurements. By this scientific method Tom learned to be quite adept at mazes and could salivate when required. He didn't mind this particularly since by and large the experiments completely bypassed (and thus didn't interfere with) his thinking.

On the other hand the second group sought to bring about an adjustment by social interactions and interpersonal relationships between Tom and his fellow inmates of level two. The inmates of level two were subjected to frequent testing and retesting. A peculiar thing was observed. The more time Tom spent with the inmates the stronger they seemed to become. It was not a matter of their being healthier exactly (particularly those who couldn't cope—their tests showed even worse antisocial traits) but rather more like their being at peace or satisfied.

When asked to account for this Tom explained it as simple: he just said out loud what most of them couldn't bear to think about. They had felt guilty for even the tendency. The reeducators viewed this with alarm since the stable inmates were less and less amenable to behavior modification and hence less likely to mentally reach the statistical tolerances for the norm that would allow their reintegration into society. Tom was disruptive and destructive as well as untrainable. They would refer the matter to the highest authority for disposition.

Quen's next to last visit was private since the highest authority, the Region Chief, hadn't visited the asylum yet and the reeducators didn't know what to do. Tom was resigned about the future. He expected to be put to death—the ultimate solution.

There is so much left to learn, to do, he told Quen with a sigh. The more I learn the more I see there is to learn. The more I see the more I understand that the impediments to sight were of our own making. The fog of confusion and despair and uselessness was cleverly created by the use of our own goodwill, our refusal to credit that things could be as they are.

Take the school system: things weren't really incredible; we were incredulous. Consider cause and effect. I found no single facilitator or educator who would say that the purpose of the system was to turn off the student, yet that was the effect. I could never shake the impression that the effect was intended but in some way so vague that it couldn't be called a conspiracy since that presumed a specific purpose formed and communicated. Admittedly it's an article of homos faith that there is no cause and effect relationship, especially in the realm of thought. At first I thought they just practice what they preach. It certainly had its effect. But now I'm beginning to see that the effect had its cause and the cause was neither natural nor accidental.

I think it's probable that there's not much time left. Bring Johnny. I want to see him one more time.

Tom was to see Johnny one more time but first he had another visitor: the Region Chief. The Region Chief was an immensely popular figure about his home region. He was to be seen everywhere doing good for those less fortunate than himself, giving away vast amounts of his family fortune as well as originating vast public works projects. Who could object to taxation in the face of such selflessness? One of his favorite causes was the poor afflicted inmates of the asylum. To bring meaning to their mindless lives he instituted therapy programs and to society's surprise and delight the inmates were found to have considerable natural or native skills in design and music.

Their primitive paintings and sculpture were, the Region Chief declared, works of art, at one and the same time primordial and prescient. The works of art were collected by the best homos. This was considered proper since it provided income to the asylum. It also created jobs and benefits in other areas. For instance, art dealers and art critics were needed to direct homos to the meaningful works. After all, the difference between a painting charged with dialectic power and junk was subtle but important. Jobs were also created when the Region Chief put up a matching endowment for the Region Chief's Museum of Modern Art. In this, as in other areas, many homos had reason to feel the effects of the Region Chief's charity.

The musical inmates had their effect, too. If it was less profound, it was more pervasive, especially among the young of homosland. The quarry bands were to be found everywhere. The success of some of these bands

caused a crisis among sociologists. None of them could determine why one band was better than another. At first it was thought to be a matter of decibels, but after all bands conformed that obviously wasn't the answer. The volume and monotony was seen to have a numbing effect and put the listeners in spiritual tune with the performers. It was called elemental or primitive and basic to homos nature. Since the music had no tune or melody the mind didn't need to grasp any form. Nobody whistled quarry tunes, lamented one old-timer. Somebody else pointed out that the lyrics weren't sung independently either although all would chant the sounds when the music started. Due to imprinting, the sociologists explained, recall having become a discredited (and unnecessary) technique since that also required form and substance.

The problem of Tom Eagle presented no difficulty to the Region Chief who after all was one of the elite performers of the establishment and one of the finest products of its educational system. As an educated and powerful homo he took instant and total aversion to Tom Eagle. It became the Region Chief's principal concern to remake Tom Eagle.

How good he is to spend his important time on the poorest of creatures, said the guards, the Head Keeper, and the PR man who arranged for the Head Keeper to be interviewed. And so said all of society, except Quen who knew who the poorest of creatures was.

We must rid his mind of its sickness, said the Region Chief. The strongest purgative we have is shock therapy. Accordingly, Tom was unchained from his

56

wall, strapped onto the therapy table, and administered electrical shocks through electrodes placed on his temples beneath an elastic band wrapped around his head. Afterward, though groggy, Tom had to be rechained to be kept from taking his own life.

It was after the third of a dozen such purgatives that Johnny and Quen managed to visit Tom. They had continually been denied access since the intervention of the Region Chief but had managed surreptitiously to penetrate the upper level. Quen was discovered because she was part animal in appearance and thrown down to the middle level from whence it was presumed she had wandered. Johnny stayed on level one where his humanoid appearance gave him protective coloration once he put a vacant expression on his face and in his eyes.

With the cooperation of ten of Tom's friends (who couldn't cope), on the night before Tom's fourth treatment, Quen smuggled Johnny down to the middle level for a private visit with his father.

When Tom saw Johnny appear before him he broke down and cried deep racking sobs that convulsed his body almost like the electric shocks. However to the worried Quen's relief they seemed to have the opposite effect.

Johnny, spoke Tom, longing to return the hug of his son but prohibited by his spread and pinioned arms from doing so. I never meant you to see me like this.

By "like this" he didn't mean in chains but disorganized. The shocks had had their effect, leaving Tom confused. They were timed to correspond with Tom's recuperative powers (resistance, the therapist called it). When he seemed to be finding his way out they would give him another. But the shock of seeing Johnny seemed to help focus his mind.

Listen to me, son, for we don't have long. And Tom began to talk to Johnny about words, about what they stood for, about thinking, about as many things as he could remember that he had thought about since their last conversation. At times Tom rambled and was confused but he would recognize it and would rally.

They are trying to scramble and disconnect the contents of my mind, he told Johnny. If what I say doesn't make sense take it home and sort it out. Don't use it unless it fits and don't use it unless you personally know or understand the basis for the remarks I've made, many of which are the conclusions of long chains of reasoning. Check your premises, Johnny Eagle. My understanding is not yours until you make it so. There is no revealed word, no shortcut to learning. Each of us must do it for himself. We have to understand everything ourselves, but we don't have to rediscover everything ourselves. Remember, first comes understanding; then comes discovery. Goodbye—always remember, I love you. Now go and give me some time with your mother.

Tom's friends of the middle level successfully spirited Quen and Johnny away before daybreak though several brave fellows were killed when they created a necessary diversion. The survivors communicated their success to Tom as he was being taken to the treatment

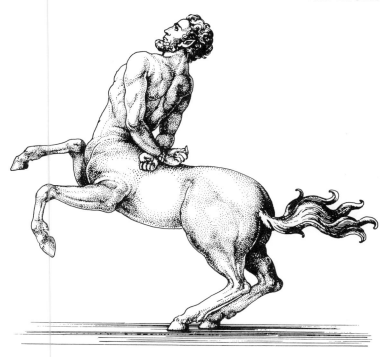

A Brave Friend of Tom

room. He smiled his thanks to each of them. It was his last volitional act.

When Tom completed the shock sequence the Region Chief declared Tom's brain empty (it wasn't really; more rendered chaotic) and eligible for retraining.

As a prominent project of the Region Chief Tom remained a public spectacle. He was taken to level one where he could be seen and rechained to the wall. His reeducators applied themselves diligently. During their rest periods Tom had to listen to the bands practice. Combined with his treatment, this unremitting assault soon allowed the reeducators to report progress. When at last his animalification had been completed the Region Chief accepted congratulations and washed his hands of Tom Eagle, suggesting that on a probationary basis he could be admitted back to society with his tribe's approval.

While the tribe spokespersons discussed terms of probation Tom, now virtually an eagle as were others of his species, found that his animalification allowed him to slip out of his chains. Summoning the last of his courage and reserves, without thinking, he flew off toward Quen and Johnny.

News of his escape, the first ever, was rapidly sounded. This galvanized the Eagle tribe who sent the swiftest and fiercest of their species to intercept Tom Eagle.

Tom Eagle was struck and killed in mid-air and his body flown over the Capitol and the countryside in the talons of two carrier eagles as an object lesson to homoskind and a demonstration of the loyalty of the eagle species. When they finished Tom's body was flown over his former retreat and dropped at the feet of Quen and Johnny Eagle.

This event had a profound effect upon Johnny Eagle. He and his mother buried the remains of his father. Johnny never uttered a word. He withdrew to his father's favorite waterfall and pool and thought about life and death; about his father's life and death; and about his, Johnny's, life.

His mother, who had watched him from a distance, met him when he returned and shared with him the grief he had denied himself while thinking. After that brief celebration she turned to him and asked: And now?

And now we go to work. Father didn't die because he knew too much; he died because he knew too little.

The first thing Johnny and Quen did was to take stock of themselves and their situation. They assessed their present circumstances and how they had arrived there, enumerating both the strengths and weaknesses of their lives. They sought the roots of their strengths and of their weaknesses. By chasing causal connections back to primary bedrock, to non-contradictory basics, they were to discover that some of their supposed weaknesses were strengths and some of their supposed strengths were weaknesses. But this didn't happen all at once.

What did happen right away was their removal to The Polis, a vast ruin that either had been or was the epitome of evil in the world. Nobody knew and nobody talked about it. It was viewed with superstition. Homoskind had not in the memory of the oldest creatures been known to penetrate The Polis. Generations previously entry had been forbidden. Perhaps it still was in the sense that the old law might still stand. That none entered was, however, not because of the law but because it never occurred to any to do so. Why would one when tribe or family, as the species were coming to be called, were not to be found there. Life outside the family was literally unthinkable, or at least none of

the homos thought of it. The most sacred birthright of every homo was his sense of identity, not only with his family (tribe, species), but with the family of homos. Great solace was to be found in the realization that all other creatures shared one's existence in a world of hardship, oppression, and evil.

But one homo did think of living outside the family: Johnny Eagle. The thought literally crossed his mind. When it did, he brought it back and examined it.

What's wrong with that thought: "One homo did think of living outside the family." It's inaccurate, but where is the inaccuracy? Surely I did so think. No con-

Creatures (Ordinary) of the Family of Homo

tradiction exists there. He thought some more and hypothesized: Maybe the contradiction is that I am not homo. But if I am not, what am I?

This problem vexed him considerably. He did not immediately find the right answer for he, too, even considering his special upbringing, was a creature of his times in that it was enormously difficult for him to subject the beliefs of his time, his culture, to fundamental reexamination.

But Johnny was more the child of his father than of his time, a fact which he identified early in consideration of the vexatious problem: What am I? That it was a problem was no problem because he had quickly learned that problems brought challenge and challenge, activity. Indeed he seldom felt more keen or alive than when confronting a problem. Johnny had learned he could prove a sum by adding a column of figures up as well as down; he could prove a subtraction problem by adding the answer to the subtrahend. He learned that he could prove the answer to a division (rapid subtraction) problem by multiplying (rapid addition) the quotient by the divisor (plus remainder, if any).

Johnny began to problem test. He was alive with problems. He could look inward and see that. He decided to look outward. He began his explorations. He had no problem finding creatures who avoided problems; almost any homo would do. He noticed they were always tired; they seemed to believe they would never get ahead; what's the use; life was unreal.

Johnny ran back to Quen. His sums added up, proved out. How exciting! Life, like arithmetic, works! Johnny would regularly sink himself in study and then come to Quen and announce he was about to go on a foray to problem test again. Quen always wanted to know where he intended to go and how long be gone. She understood his need to reality test his theories but was never easy while he was gone.

One day Johnny discovered that numbers came from real things. They stood for something in reality, anything specific in reality, as 1 rock, 2 clouds, etc. It was as though the first creature to count had kept tally on his digits. That he knew where numbers came from wasn't what was exciting, he explained to Quen. That numbers were labels: that was what was exciting. They were names or noms or nouns. Suppose *all* words were names for something!

He came back later: Or for actions!

Or for relationships, he said, dashing in and out again.

And then . . . and then he came very solemnly back to Quen. Father said it was all in the words. Words are labels. They stand for something, something specific in reality, he said. Something that exists. I exist. . . .

I am. I am means I—me—Johnny Eagle—exist. I am what I am—not more, not less. I am. Johnny Eagle is . . . the thinking animal.

Yes, you are, said Quen, regarding her offspring with . . . with love? Yes, but . . . with respect? Yes, but still not quite . . . with . . . a difference. She had no word for it.

You are different, Johnny Eagle. And I love you more because of it, she added. She smiled in pleasure as she saw Johnny suffused with pleasure.

Preen wasn't the right word, she thought, as she remembered their discussion later when Johnny retreated to his favorite thinking place.

Johnny approached her several days later quite shaken.

What is the matter, Quen wanted to know.

I almost lost it, Johnny told her. I was so enamored of the thinking animal that I thought: I think therefore I am. I believe, therefore I exist—a credo.

Creatures Who Thought They Existed

It's incredible, he said. That's exactly backward. I exist, a creature possessing reason, therefore I think; not the other way around.

Suppose I thought poorly, or not at all? he asked.

Then you would be a snox or an eleoxen, laughed Quen.

Well, figuratively perhaps, Johnny laughed, his tension broken. But not actually. Actually any creature can learn or not learn or dislearn; but in the space of one life span one cannot create himself a snox or an eleoxen. That's an evolutionary process and it has taken them generation upon generation to get this far; though, he smiled at Quen, they do seem to be speeding the process. Perhaps the process proceeds geometrically rather than arithmetically, he thought out loud.

In any case, the important thing is what can one learn or, a better word, know. One can't know what isn't, what is non-existent. If it doesn't exist, it's nothing. If it exists, it's something. If it is something, it has identity. If it has identity it is knowable.

If it has no identity it is nothing, observed Quen, caught up with the chain. She continued: If it is nothing, it doesn't exist. If it doesn't exist, has no identity, it is unknowable.

Yes, agreed Johnny, but don't forget to distinguish between the unknown and the unknowable. The unknown exists but we don't understand it yet. The unknowable can never exist.

If it exists it is a part of the totality of existence we call nature. If it exists we may perceive and understand its nature, its identity.

Then if it is above, beyond, or outside of nature, it is supranatural?

Right! The supranatural doesn't now, never did, and never can exist. It is unknowable. It is without identity. It is nothing. As such it can have no reality in the world; only in the mind of a thinking animal.

Yes, of course. And thinking won't make it so or make it existentially real. It would only be subjective. Quen paused. Suppose people thought they were ghosts? That wouldn't make them so?

No, replied Johnny. But consider that the *concept* of ghosts *can be,* for there is no guarantee that all thought will be accurate or consistent with that which is, with existence. The state of your mind is real, like the state of your stomach. A sick concept, like a stomach ache, may, though intangible, exist in a creature possessing capacity to experience it. In this sense, while ghosts, the supranatural, cannot create man, man can create ghosts or any other form of irrationality.

Then concepts can be right or wrong, reflected Quen.

Right. We give a label to all concepts since they exist . . . as concepts. But they may or may not refer to actual things, to existents. They may be consistent with that which is and true or they may be unconnected to reality and false. An unconnected or floating concept or idea can be learned but when learned isn't knowledge. Knowledge is learning that is consistent with reality, truth.

What is learning *not* consistent with reality? asked Quen.

Creatures Who Did Exist Possessing Some Degree of Awareness

Garbage! said Johnny, his vehemence a reflection of his prior emotional experience. And that's what really scared me. When I have a stomach ache, I automatically know it, but it seems a mind-ache doesn't happen automatically. In fact, it seems I could abuse or perhaps poison my mind and not know it. The faculty that processes and digests food is the stomach. The faculty that processes and digests information is the mind.

It has just dawned on me how important it is to be aware or conscious of what one feeds the mind. Such awareness obviously is not automatic. If I wish to be aware, I must choose to be so. I am free to be or not to be purposely conscious, focused.

The snoxes and eleoxen have tried and tried to free us of this freedom. They have tried to make knowledge automatic and to some extent they have succeeded . . . for them. That's why they hated Father, because he was different, because he didn't want automatic knowledge.

That's what makes me different, Mother. I am a creature of volitional consciousness.

I choose to think. I am a homo, genus Homo, but I exist thinking, not automatically but volitionally. That being so, I have the freedom to learn and know, or learn and not know, or not learn at all. In the latter two cases I or my progeny would sooner or later come into conflict with reality and die out. If I learn and know, think effectively, I exist sapient. I am Homo sapiens, the knowledgeable animal—who lives . . . and prospers.

With these fundamental identifications Johnny Eagle set about to control and remake his world to his comfort and his satisfaction.

He soon found out that there were two key elements to success: knowledge and knowledge applied. Think and Do, said Johnny.

In his pursuit of knowledge there was no place too sacred or profane for Johnny to go. He penetrated to the very heart of The Polis and made frequent excursions into the surrounding homosland. He never thought to hide himself because occasionally he would meet some interesting creature and they would animatedly talk the day and night away. Several creatures joined him as a result of these conversations. Although they were few in number Johnny was quick to grasp the potential of competence feeding back upon itself. Give me ten good, strong-minded fellows . . . , he once speculated to Quen.

Quen was always nervous about Johnny's forays and her apprehensions were justified one day when one of Johnny's fellows came running up to the school shouting, Quen! Quen! They've arrested Johnny!

Part the Second

. . . SUBJECT TO CHOICE . . .

Chapter IV

THE TRIAL OF JOHNNY EAGLE

JOHNNY EAGLE, YOU ARE brought before the Council of The Ultimate to answer the most serious charge of blasphemy of The Ultimate; further, to answer for high crimes of antisocial behavior; and, finally, for various misdemeanors resulting from acts and conduct detrimental to the public welfare.

How do you plead?

By whose yardstick or standard am I to plead? asked Johnny.

Silence. You are not permitted to ask questions, admonished the Prosecutor. My Lords, he convicts himself from his own mouth. Every citizen knows questions are the sole prerogative of The Ultimate and its properly constituted agencies, such as Your Worships at this Tribunal.

Very well, said Johnny, by my own standard I plead Not Guilty.

Now we have him, pathetic child, how could he

feel he could face the power of The Ultimate, thought the Prosecutor.

And is your standard different than that of homoskind? asked one judge.

Do you mean as promulgated in the name of homos or as necessitated by his nature? asked Johnny.

Silence! You are not permitted to ask questions! shouted the Prosecutor.

According to the law of the land, responded the Judge.

My standard is that required by the nature of any individual homo, stated Johnny.

Is that the law of the land?

No, it is a standard dictated only by the law of identity, said Johnny.

You are trying to confuse us, said the Judge. Do you honor and obey the law of the land? Say yes or no.

Yes or no, said Johnny.

Blasphemy! exclaimed the Prosecutor. He mocks The Ultimate in the persons of Your Worships.

I did not intend so, said Johnny. By "No" I meant that I infringed or intruded upon no homo except by principle of mutual consent. I state my basis of existence and do not deal with my fellow homo if he exists on another basis, at least as regards his dealings with me. By "Yes" I meant that my private life is lived contrary to the law of the land. Thus I honor your right to live your life as you see fit but obey my own right to live life as I see fit.

You are confusing me, said a Judge. You mean you honor your own life but do not obey the Law.

No, say rather, I do not disobey the law.

How can you do that? interrupted the Prosecutor.

By living alone, said Johnny.

That's against the law, said the Prosecutor.

No, it isn't, said Johnny. So far you haven't passed that law. Thousands of homos live alone, symbolically, in parts of their lives. I do so substantially in the whole of mine.

That's not so, said the Judge. You are here now. Now you are not alone. How can you say so?

I live alone by choice. I am not here by choice. I was brought here, said Johnny.

You lie, said the Prosecutor, on two counts. First, it is the nature of homoskind to need one another, and even though you are a poor example of the species, you share that need; and secondly, you lied because you do in fact share your existence with others. We are reliably informed that there are at least ten or twelve students at your school besides yourself and your mother.

No, I do not lie, said Johnny. Need is an ambiguous word. You use it to connote weakness and reliance; one homo needs another. If, however, you view homo as fundamentally strong and self-reliant, you will find that such individuals by their individualistic nature can accomplish more by association with other individuals, whether in terms of production (creativity) or consumption (enjoyment). Such associations, based on strength as man's nature, have a proper basis. Because the strong grow stronger, one could say there was a need for association. If you wish to know whether an

We Are Confused

association or a society is proper, tell me whether it is based on strength or weakness.

Here he will be tripped into an overt blasphemy, thought a judge.

We are confused, the Prosecutor and a deputy prompted.

Are you saying our society is weak? asked the judge.

I am not accountable or on trial for your actions, said Johnny; only for mine. My society is strong.

You are not answering our questions, screamed the Prosecutor.

I am sorry, said Johnny. I thought I was. If I have not been doing so, I shall try harder.

Yes, yes, go on, said the Chief Judge. Forget the blasphemy charge; go on to the High Crimes, he directed the Prosecutor, while glancing at the TV camera for, while books, newspapers, and the printed word had fallen from general to total disuse, the oral society of homos depended very heavily on their TV's (if only they didn't keep breaking down, thought the judge, relieved to see the red light was on).

Rise, Johnny Eagle, lower your head, and hear the bill of particulars enumerating your high crimes, said the Prosecutor (sneaking a look, seeing that Johnny Eagle had risen, and hurrying on):

1. Entering the Polis, for which no useful public purpose exists and to no public benefit;
2. Stealing children and poisoning their minds, thereby depriving homoskind of the benefit of their labors;

3. Questioning and arguing in public, both acts useless and therefore wasteful of the gross national public productivity;
4. Failing to submit yourself to the teachings of homoskind to learn animalification; and lastly,
5. Failing to confess your errors and submit yourself to the tribal, regional, or national System of Homos Family Justice.

How do you plead to these charges of High Crime?

Not Guilty, said Johnny.

Do you deny the acts giving rise to these charges? questioned a judge.

No, stated Johnny. On the underlying facts we are in agreement.

Then how can you plead Not Guilty? asked the Chief Judge.

My father was killed because he asked the question, Why should one homo live for another? He found the answer and consequence at the same time: death. He was a creature who sought to live for himself in a world that didn't. The ultimate extension of life for another is death. The ultimate sacrifice is death. The end and goal of your morality is death. You kill yourselves by parts, by compromise, by sacrifice. If you don't have something of value, your cannot sacrifice it. If you don't have something of value, you cannot compromise it. When you encountered a creature who refused to be killed by parts you killed the whole. The whole you killed, the value that wouldn't sacrifice or compromise, was life.

You tell homos that their world is evil. The great

irony is that you are right. It is your world and you and every other creature make it what it is—for yourselves. Existence in this sense is neuter. It will be what you make of it. You are free to consider or think it twisted and distorted in any way you please. What you are not free to do is escape the consequences of your consideration or thinking.

You seek to act as a mass, a body, an entity and thereby escape the consequences of individual existence. The essence of my so-called crimes is that I acted individually. I freely state that I did. My actions are the consequences, the effects, of a cause: I am an individual. That I know so is the effect of having reasoned effectively. The consequence of knowledge is, was, and will be that the sapient animal—**MAN** is his name—will remake the world to his purposes.

You ask how do I plead Not Guilty to homos justice. Because I am man.

Your justice does not apply to me. What you seek to evade is that just as existence exists, justice exists. It can be inaccurately perceived, but what it is is: it cannot be faked, conned, twisted, or distorted—not by wishes, not by prayers, not by guns, not by torture, not by laws or even by death. Justice is existence lived. Properly it is life as man. We each get justice; we get that which is our due; even in irrational times or times of irrationality, most especially, if not most clearly, do we get justice.

Why do I plead Not Guilty? Guilty of what? That, typically unhomo, I won't be conned existentially into working so that those who con me can be paid with my taxes? That I won't believe or have faith so that those who con me spiritually can be paid with my charity?

Does it surprise you that I have charity? Then why do you constantly appeal to it? Doesn't it strike you as ludicrous that I give charity but am uncharitable—because I don't pay more; that I pay taxes but am unpatriotic—because I don't pay more.

Let me tell you something. By your standards: I am unpatriotic; I am uncharitable. Even more basic than that: I am unhomo. I am man.

I am the conceptual animal who refuses to pay more because he was conceived in original sin, because he lives sinfully, or so that others may do so. I am not weak. My nature is not base. I have no need to inherit the earth. It is mine—now. And the sooner I realize it, the more responsibly will I behave toward it.

While I am not guilty, neither am I innocent, not in the sense you mean. I have been in and of the world and learned. Some learning was erroneous. I learned from that. All that resulted in knowledge, whether easy or hard-won, was and is the stuff of life. Every creature must learn the lessons appropriate for the survival of his species. As the creature man it pleases me to say thanks to my intellectual parents, whether living or dead, for their lessons. As they would understand, now it's up to me.

I am the creature of intellect. My means of survival is reason. I am the conceptual animal. I am knowledgeable. I am Homo sapiens. I am human. I am man.

I am not guilty.

There was a silence when Johnny Eagle finished. It was as though most of the homos didn't wish to break it and the rest didn't dare to.

But the Chief Judge did.

Just more words, Johnny Eagle. Any fool can use words. They have been discredited for years. They are no basis for action.

What is? asked Johnny.

Well, everybody knows. You don't have to state it. Some things are too pure to be profaned by words. You are not in tune with homos vibrations, Johnny Eagle. If you don't understand, no explanation is possible. If you do understand, no explanation is necessary.

I understand, said Johnny Eagle, which means explanation is possible. If I bore you goodwill it would mean that explanation was . . .

Stop! cried the Chief Judge as his fellow judges herded toward him. That cry echoed and reverberated across homosland prompting the Chief Judge to challenge, You are at *our* mercy! What good are your concepts? He glanced right and left along the bench, but not at the TV.

My concepts are my method, as man, of meeting problems. The general problem of man is to understand he is man. The special problem of man is to live like one, Johnny answered.

The Chief Judge was handed a note.

The Court will take a ten minute recess, he announced, and pounded his gavel. The Court in recess heard from the snox opinion samplers that the

The Cry "Stop" Echoed and Reverberated Across Homosland

TV audience, never higher, was upset and restless.

We will need a strategem, said the Snox Chief, and proceeded to set it forth.

When the Court reconvened the Chief Judge said:

Johnny Eagle, stand forward and hear the judgment of the Court. You are found guilty of all charges brought against you.

There was among the spectators a murmur that began to swell ominously for reasons they themselves couldn't account.

Silence in the courtroom, repeated the Chief Judge. Listen to the wisdom of The Ultimate. As the noise subsided he continued.

Johnny Eagle, because of your tender years the Court has decided in spite of your guilt to be merciful in its sentence. That all may understand the quality of mercy . . . he paused, looked at the assembly and into the TV cameras, then dramatically resumed . . . we hereby sentence you to the following punishment. You shall in mercy be neither put to death nor incarcerated (at which much of the tension went out of the courtroom and viewing audience). But you shall be condemned to live the life you seem to espouse. You shall be forbidden the society of homoskind. You are cast out into the darkness. You are expelled from the garden of civilization and shall henceforth bear the pain and consequences of your impertinences. Any homos having intercourse with you or your associates, who are also guilty by association, shall suffer the same penalty.

Furthermore, hear this: this sentence is subject to

85

review. It is our belief that you will fail and crawl back as the consequences of your words are borne out. Be advised that you will get no further mercy from this Court and that the Court will review the sentence as hereafter provided.

You are directed to report back to this tribunal nine years hence when you reach majority at 21 for further trial, at which time your age will not protect you. Because of your statements of strength before this tribunal, be advised that at that time you may expect no mercy to be shown. Be further advised that the continuation of this trial shall, by the most honorable standards of justice, be, in your own terms, a test of strength; that is—trial by ordeal. It shall be a contest of strength between homoskind and Johnny Eagle. You will be prohibited to conduct your defense with your tricky use of words. Such is the judgment of The Ultimate. Do you wish to object or appeal to the Court?

No, said Johnny. To object would be ineffective; to appeal, inconsistent. Let it stand.

Then let it be so promulgated. Such is the mercy of The Ultimate, pronounced the Chief Judge, and pounded his gavel.

Everyone agreed that The Ultimate was most merciful, especially those who felt, whether with upset or with glee, that Johnny had been about to die. Everyone, that is, except a few homos for reasons they couldn't give, and Johnny for reasons he could.

I neither asked for nor received mercy, he said. Mercy is that given in suspense of or contradiction to justice. Their sentence of outcast is what I practice

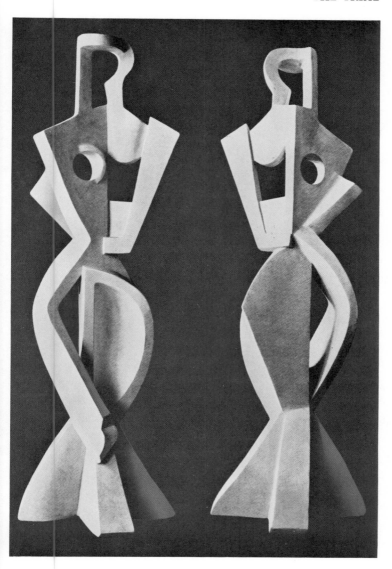

Two Snox Acolytes Discussing the Sentence

without their sanction; in that sense it was justice, not mercy, though they did not intend it so.

With his fellow students, he returned to his wilderness not to be heard from in the intervening nine years, during which time the world largely forgot Johnny Eagle.

Chapter V

THE LABORS OF JOHNNY EAGLE

IN FACT, THE WORLD might have completely forgotten about Johnny Eagle except that, true to his word, on his 21st birthday he presented himself to the Council of The Ultimate for the continuation of his trial.

What transpired in the intervening nine years, said the old turtle, was anyone's guess. Anything that did happen must be inferred. Some said Johnny Eagle made a pact with the Devil; Black Magic was a common subsequent explanation. Many said he discovered the fountain of youth because when the tribunal reconvened Johnny Eagle was still a mere youth and the judges still living had aged visibly. Of course the judges' wisdom could not be doubted because everyone knows the older the doctrine and its spokesmen the greater its validity.

In any case, the Council of The Ultimate met to discuss the problem of Johnny Eagle. We must have a trial, said the Chief Eleoxen. We have promised the homos one. He presented himself only yesterday and already they talk of nothing else.

Let's just kill him and be done with it, said Eleoxen Six.

No, said the snox counselors. You must not make a martyr of him. What we must do is humiliate him. We must take this opportunity to show the superiority of our system.

That shouldn't be hard, said the Chief. We remember that this is to be trial by ordeal. He is forbidden to argue or confuse us with his words. He is therefore impotent. The Chief Judge became more confident as he talked.

Yes, without his words Johnny Eagle is nearly powerless, rejoined the Snox Chief.

He is frail without being fleet, said another snox.

His substance is without strength, added still another.

True, enthused the Chief. In all justice then, we must expose Johnny Eagle's nature to homoskind. But the question is how?

Why not let our best homos show their superiority over Johnny Eagle? said the snox.

How do you mean? asked the Chief.

Let him compete against our best runners, our best pullers, our best . . .

Yes, yes, interrupted the Chief, much taken with the idea. He doesn't stand a chance. We shall try him justly, *then* kill him, he admonished Eleoxen Six.

It will be very instructive, said Snox Nine.

It will be very entertaining! said Eleoxen Thirteen, quick to join in now that the drift of the Council was determined.

What a pity our TV no longer works, said the Chief. All the world could witness and learn and enjoy the humiliation of Johnny Eagle.

Yes, that is lamentable, agreed the Snox Chief. Perhaps we could accomplish the same effect by having the trials moved from place to place within the country.

We like it, said the Chief. We shall have one contest or trial between homoskind and Johnny Eagle on each new moon for the next twelve moons, to be at sites selected by the snoxes and against the finest homos of our land.

The Council signified its unanimous consensus with a roar of approval. Well, Eleoxen Six did growl a little about a big waste of time.

To implement the consensus, it was promulgated throughout the land by public criers that on the next twelve new moons at certain sites there would be trial by contest, homoskind versus Johnny Eagle.

Imagine what excitement this caused. In fact, it caused so much excitement so immediately that the Council decided it would be desirable to take out some insurance on the outcome.

It must be no holds barred, said Eleoxen Six, and, for once in agreement with Eleoxen Six, the Snox Chief added that it should be a unanimous verdict to find him not guilty, that is, he must win all twelve contests or suffer death.

The Chief (Eleoxen) (Judge)

Agreed, said they all, though all wished the Snox Chief would have not mentioned not guilty. It was somehow disquieting to have this introduced.

There is a delegation of citizens here from various regions, each clamoring for the privilege of hosting the trials, the sentinel informed the Council.

Then, said the Chief, it must be the twelve largest regions for maximum exposure.

Yes, interposed the snox; but there is great rivalry for the first and early positions since it is generally held that there may not be more than one test.

We shall reward the regions in order, according to their support of the Council, said the Chief to general agreement.

But what about Johnny Eagle? said Eleoxen 27. Has anybody asked him?

Told him, said Eleoxen Six. If he doesn't like it, kill him now.

The Chief ordered that Johnny Eagle be brought before the Council.

Johnny Eagle, said the Snox Chief, you stand arraigned before the Council assembled. How do you plead, guilty or not guilty?

Forget that, said the Chief Judge, remembering the last trial. This is a trial or contest, Johnny Eagle, whereby the Council in its infinite justice has determined that you shall pit your skills against homoskind. Your endeavors shall be measured against the endeavors of our culture. If you are found wanting, you shall die. If you are unequal to the tasks, you shall die.

If you object, you shall die now, said Eleoxen Six.

Do you agree? continued the Chief Judge.

Yes, said Johnny Eagle.

The Snox Chief said, do you understand that it takes a unanimous result to establish your innocence?

Yes, said Johnny Eagle.

Do you understand that it is no holds barred, anything goes? said Eleoxen Six.

Yes, said Johnny Eagle, who of course had heard or had reported the proclamations of the criers.

Then so be it! decreed the Chief. In the name of the Council, let it be promulgated amongst the homos of our land that at the following sites the following contests of strength shall take place between homoskind and Johnny Eagle.

And thus began the twelve labors of Johnny Eagle.

The first was a contest of speed. Great debate ensued as to who should represent the homos in Capitol Region. The snoxes actually wanted a relatively slow animal such as a rabbithomo to be the contestant on the grounds that if the contest were won by the least of the homo creatures, the greater the victory; and if it weren't won, then the second region would have a chance for a contest at no substantial loss of face.

Persuaded by the arguments that all who could should see the contests, the Chief Judge declared each trial day to be a national holiday, whereby any citizen could have the day off work to attend the trial. Such a commotion. A day off work. Homoskind had worked from sun-up to sun-down for so long that the young believed it only a myth that it was ever otherwise. A national holiday, why that was as good as a Snoxday, which occurred once every seven, and for which all were grateful.

Johnny Eagle can't be all bad, said some of the young irreverent homos as they set out for Capitol Region. The only complaint heard was from those of distant cities who couldn't come to view and return in one day. Since it was out of the question that they should be allowed additional days for travel (they would never meet their quotas), it was decided on the principle of equality to make the holiday apply even to those who couldn't attend the trial.

To the snoxes' great satisfaction, this had the effect, as their opinion samplers reported back, of making the Council very popular. When relayed, this struck the Council as a very just characterization and reaffirmed their opinions of the collective wisdom of homoskind.

To the snoxes' further great satisfaction, the opinion samplers also reported back that many homos were rooting for Johnny Eagle so that there would be more than one national holiday. Of course the snoxes did not report to the Council this effect of its decision. Rather they used the example to instruct young snoxes that homo is basically selfish and evil and, without explicitly saying so, made them understand that as long as homos expressed their admiration for the ideal and practiced something else they would always need snoxes to remind them what was proper.

Naturally the Chief of Capitol Region had no intention of seeing his region and its members lose face. He wouldn't even compromise on a horsehomo. It would be the cheetahhomo versus Johnny Eagle.

And so it came to pass on the day of the race that before a great assemblage there appeared all the dignitaries of homosland as well as Capitol Region and also Johnny Eagle and his band of a hundred odd-looking creatures.

How ugly they are. They seem to have no grace, said one lively, flippant young thing. They look like overgrown babies except that some have partially developed wings or tails or other anatomical aberrations, murmured others.

It was considered instructive by the snoxes to expose this retardation to the masses to provide an object lesson. One could be strong as a tunahomo or beautiful as a nightingalehomo, but to be neither fishhomo nor fowlhomo was a terrible thing; and so thought they all, grateful to have the grace to be one or the other or something else.

The myriad supporters and trainers of the cheetahhomo gathered about their candidate prior to the start of the race.

The one hundred supporters and trainers of Johnny Eagle, which consisted of his mother and his friends and classmates from school, gathered around him.

Both contestants were called to the starting line. The course, a simple one-mile cinder oval, laid out before the grandstands was described to the contestants.

The winner's circle and the guillotine were pointed

out to the contestants and by megaphone to the assembled throng. Any who couldn't hear were informed by word of mouth from those who could or who were in turn so informed.

Everyone wanted to know about the controversy which developed just prior to the start of the race. As best those distant could get it, it seemed that Johnny Eagle had a device he called a machine that he brought with him. It seemed a snox objected but Johnny called on Eleoxen Six to bear witness that it was a contest of strength with no holds barred.

Eleoxen Six looked at the so-called machine and saw how heavy it was. He pushed it and saw that it didn't roll easily even though it had wheels.

Johnny Eagle said his strength was in his mind; that he was the thinking animal; and, since no holds were barred, he was free to use his mind or strength as he saw fit.

The Chief Judge ruled (after giving weight to the arguments of the snox and of Eleoxen Six) that Eleoxen Six was right, that Johnny Eagle, the thinking animal, could use his ridiculous machine if he wished to so handicap himself.

At the starting line Johnny Eagle kicked a lever and his machine began to make the most terrible racket. It scared not only his fellow contestant, but most of the rest of the homos nearby. However, as Johnny Eagle stepped astride his machine, confidence returned.

How can anyone run like that? they said. The great noise is just to scare us.

Get ready; get set; go! said the starter and, true to

expectations, the cheetahhomo was off at a lightning clip. Indeed, the cheetahhomo's confidence rose with his clean, quick start. The infernal machine was, he could tell by the noise, left behind. There only remained to settle into a steady lope to finish first. By the quarter pole he could tell the machine was still a long way back. By the half-way mark, could he hear it growing closer? By the three-quarter pole the racket had drawn up next to him, both scaring and spurring him on to greater effort. He had never run so fast and yet now he needn't hear Johnny Eagle; he could see him pulling away and crossing the finish line ahead. Moments afterward the cheetahhomo collapsed yards short of the finish line.

The crowd went wild.

It's only because they want another holiday, said the snoxes. Spread the word; it's only because they want another holiday.

Johnny Eagle was inundated by his followers and by a large number of homos as he brought the machine back to the starting line. (Many of the homos were to remark afterwards to their children and grandchildren that they had touched him and he was not unhomo.)

Johnny Eagle made no effort to head for the victory circle, where the Chief Eleoxen and the Snox Chief were waiting sullenly, but sought out his fellow contestant.

Where is he? he asked.

Eleoxen Six took him, was the only response.

All of a sudden they heard the guillotine. Johnny was infuriated. His followers had to hold him back.

He was a noble adversary, said Johnny with tears in his eyes.

Later Eleoxen Six stated that survival of the fittest was the law of Homosland. The cheetahhomo didn't deserve to live.

Quen had quieted Johnny by telling him that the cheetahhomo had already died a few yards short of the finish.

He ran his heart out, said Johnny. We could have made a man of him.

Thereafter Johnny refused to compete against any single contestant. Because most of the homos were revolted by Eleoxen Six's actions, the condition was met.

The second contest was a test of stamina wherein Johnny, in competition with the water buffalohomo and the camelhomo, was challenged to negotiate a variety of terrain. Afterward there was considerable grumbling amongst the various establishments about Johnny's luck in choosing the load or burden he carried on his machine.

All in all a most unsatisfactory contest it was generally held. The camelhomo got bogged down in the delta and the water buffalohomo became prostrated in the desert. Johnny, who finished minus all of his load except camping equipment (the wood was consumed as rafting; the water was consumed in the desert; and the fuel and food were consumed over the distance), had to be declared the winner—by default as it were since he was the only finisher. That he did so at all was bad enough; that he did so while appearing refreshed and rested was intolerable.

Because general opinion held that the failure of the camelhomo and water buffalohomo was due to the fact that their loads had been selected unselfishly (commemorative medals and gifts for the judges) and because the camelhomo tribe and the water buffalohomo tribe had been selfish (each insisted on terrain suited to its own species), it was decided that productivity or contribution to homoanity should thenceforth be an element of the contest.

The third trial involved literally the masses in that assorted homos jointly proficient in the onerous problem of water management (cooliehomos they were called) challenged Johnny to pit himself against their brigades. Johnny's machine, called a pump, not only handled the irrigation problem more efficiently but, as Johnny explained, could reach deeper aquifiers, drain swamps, fill artificial lakes.

Stop, begged the cooliehomos, already much alarmed. Of what use could artificial lakes possibly be, they asked one another.

To make life easier, said Johnny. To have water where you want it when you want it. And for recreation.

What's recreation? their spokeshomo asked. When they were told their suspicions were confirmed: Johnny's machines were infernal devices whose purpose was to take jobs away. Without jobs who could live. It would mean an end to life as we know it, they said. Why, the street sweepers would be next! Who could guess where it would end.

Johnny came away with the victory, which pleased him, but also with the enmity of the cooliehomos and such of their spiritual brethren as they could alarm, which saddened him.

Johnny's fourth labor or contest involved agility in that the difficulty was to move a ton of boxes from the base to the top of a very high cliff. The goathomos were heavily favored. Johnny carried none of his boxes on the first trip up his trail which was for him so steep and laborious that the first goathomos were back for their second round of boxes by the time Johnny reached the top.

When he didn't reappear the crowd asked the goathomos if Johnny were resting.

No, he's building some sort of structure.

Soon the rope Johnny had carried up came snaking down and was pulled back up with a stouter rope attached. Very shortly thereafter Johnny rappelled down the cliff and connected the rope system to his driving machine.

After he ran the rope system around twice, made some adjustments, rode it up and made some adjustments at the top, he came back down and began to load boxes onto his conveyor. When they saw what was happening the goathomo tribe panicked. They threw all available goatpower into the task. Unfortunately they clogged their narrow and precarious trail so that for a while those coming down could not get down nor those up up. Johnny suggested they use his trail to return thereby setting up a traffic pattern, but even so it was clear to the assembled watchers that Johnny would finish as far ahead at the end as he had been behind at the beginning.

The judges left by twos and threes—as did most of the crowd after Johnny shut down his machine. He and his supporters were free to leave as well except that they spent considerable time explaining the system to those who wanted to know. They were further detained when they offered to transport the remaining goathomos down from the top. Soon everybody wanted a ride and the whole business took on more the appearance of a fair than a trial—even one by ordeal.

The fifth labor of Johnny Eagle transpired in Farmregion against the agrarianhomos. Johnny's task or challenge was to match the productivity of the farmerhomo, for while it was fashionable to deny or evade the substantial contribution of those who dealt directly with the land, it was, conversely, on their competence that the snoxes fell back after the first four failures. They had suspended the schedule of events in order to win.

The agrarianhomos were unused to attention. Too many times had they been attacked by consumer spokeshomos for rising prices. They regularly kept a low profile and as a result they hadn't even submitted a petition for a trial venue.

It came then as a considerable surprise when the snoxes informed them they would represent homoskind in a test of productivity. Characteristically they proceeded straightaway to deal with the matter. They proposed two forty-acre fields of cotton be selected as the test. When Johnny suggested that the area be increased to a quarter-section the fair-minded agrarianhomos asked Johnny how many sacks he wanted for his assistants. The snoxes overruled this since, while Johnny had demanded multiple opposing participants, homoskind had not been so stupid. Johnny's friends were limited to support and advice. Accordingly, amidst a considerable feeling of unfairness toward the snoxes, the agrarianhomos were ordered to proceed to trial.

The farmerhomos invited Johnny, Quen, and his fellows to a hearty farm breakfast which, as was their habit, commenced before daybreak. Their native goodwill was tinged with sadness as they discovered, breaking bread together, that these strange creatures were regular fellows—at least in attitude if not appearance.

In spite of the exhortations and threats of the snoxes the picking team refrained from entering the fields at daybreak (even though they had chosen their number to result in work completed by evening). If they had to work late, well, they frequently did. And though it went against their habit they lingered at table while their leaders encouraged Johnny to start.

Johnny agreed to start and drove an odd-looking machine toward the cotton fields. He commenced operations not on his own 80 acres but on his opponents', driving up and down the rows without regard to boundaries. As he drove back and forth the assembled crowd was at first dumbfounded and then exercised. The first reaction was that Johnny was destroying the cotton, but as they examined the plants and saw the trailer fill with cotton bols they felt instead awe, then concern as the snox councilors began their tirades. After their initial fear the agrarianhomos with characteristic common sense told the snoxes to shut up for it was apparent to all of them that Johnny would singlehandedly complete the task before lunch.

As you may imagine, lunch was a festive occasion.

While all assembled had been at the fields watching the efforts of Johnny Eagle (No! No! said the snoxes—watching The Machine) Quen and Johnny's fellows had prepared and set out a solid and substantial lunch for the agrarianhomos—whether contestants or not. Johnny and his fellows were closely pressed at lunchtime to explain the causes of the consequences all had observed. The agrarianhomos listened attentively to the reasons given.

Sensing the disequilibrium between the conditioned need to do and the budding desire to know, Johnny proposed that further discussion be adjourned from the already prolonged luncheon until after supper.

But the work is done, they said, intending to accord Johnny justice but being uneasy or ungraceful in their statement. Johnny knew, however, that for the productive creature work is never done and immediately put them at their ease inviting them, by way of holiday, to repair to the fields for a further demonstration. The further demonstration consisted of plowing, disking, fertilizing, and seeding, successively, the same quarter section. As Johnny's fellows detached one implement and attached another the avid agrarians besieged them with questions of how.

Not unnaturally, supper as well took on aspects of an occasion. Johnny promised to leave the agrarian-homos instructions for further tilling and implements for harvesting. He promised to design them a—he called it a reaper—and told them how in this region they could get a third crop.

The sixth labor arose perhaps accidentally, from that celebratory supper. The only sour note sounded had been by the Court's representatives who had felt obliged to say something. They had to acknowledge Johnny's field victory but in a bid to win the favor of the feminine agrarian contingent pointed out that the harvest was only half the story.

Johnny took up the challenge and the cotton harvest was divided in two. In the intervening month the farmerhomos wives were busy with their skills while Johnny and his fellows labored at their machines. On the appointed day when they again assembled the female agrarianhomos presented their products to Johnny, Quen, and the fellows.

Quen graciously accepted on behalf of all and acknowledged the fine workmanship which could not be duplicated (they had paid particular care). She then called the attention of the ladies and the rest of the guests to the cotton bols stored from harvest time. Johnny set in motion both the cotton gin and the instruction teams which in the course of the day not only explained the gin, but the spinner, the loom, and the sewing machines. Under Quen's direction other teams fired indoor ovens, vented by air pumps, and further processed, cooled, heated, mixed, pureed and otherwise prepared agrarian produce as well as mechanically washed and ironed the garments and fabrics fabricated that day so that once again supper was a time of . . . of giving thanks, suggested several spontaneously.

There were no representatives of the judges present at that supper.

By this time the snox and eleoxen groups were extremely upset. Things weren't working out the way they had planned at all.

Eleoxen Six told them he had told them it was all a waste of time.

He was joined in his grumblings by more of his faction this time. It was apparent to the snox faction that they were going to be blamed.

Even the Chief Eleoxen, generally amenable to the advice of his snox councilors, began to growl, complaining that there wasn't much use being a judge when there wasn't anything to judge. All in all, he reasoned, trial by ordeal was an unfair process. He liked the old system better when after both sides rested they had to turn to him (generally in fear and trepidation—although he didn't admit this) for verdict and judgment. Trial by ordeal is too objective, he concluded.

Disliking the tone of the conclave the Snox Chief conceived and immediately implemented what, after the meeting, his admiring fellows told him was his most brilliant ploy.

He told the eleoxen, We must certainly stop Johnny Eagle. He is a clear and present danger to the welfare of the realm. Our opinion samples show he exerts a considerable disruptive effect on the populace.

Our trouble heretofore, and we freely and humbly admit it, was that we allowed Johnny to contest against lesser creatures.

So? asked the eleoxen.

So, if we wish to put an end to Johnny Eagle let

him compete against the greatest of the homos—the eleoxen. Into the surprised silence the Snox Chief continued: Consider, with your ancestry, how could anyone expect to handle burdens the way you can. Your brute (oops, he thought) strength is unparalleled in our history.

His slip slid by the increasingly animated eleoxen who began individually to clamor for the right to compete against Johnny Eagle. Fights broke out. The Chief Eleoxen restored order and on advice of his private species or tribal council decreed that any or all eleoxen could participate. The next contest would be to pull a burden from one town to another ten miles distant. It was to take place at the next new moon and be no holds barred. The eleoxen contestants could select their own burdens whether bulky or compact just as long as they were heavy. He told them they could be carried, pulled, or even pushed and in any fashion—on skids or wagons or otherwise. Further, the eleoxen were free to work individually or in tandem or any other way to beat Johnny Eagle.

The seventh labor was the busiest month of the contest. The region of the country where the two towns were located was abustle with activity—on both sides. All the comings and goings furnished fodder for speculation to even the most distant inhabitants of homosland. It was clear days before the event that the biggest crowd ever would assemble; and indeed, when the day arrived, their numbers were too great for any to see more than a portion of the contest. Some of the early arrivals chose the staging area at town A and others the finish line at town B. Most had to choose something in between so they lined the roadway on both sides, in some cases many homos deep as late arrivals from distant places kept adding to the throng. What a day!

At the staging area the Court passed in review, pausing from time to time to inspect the burdens or arrangements of some individual or team of eleoxen, wishing them well and godspeed. When they passed before Johnny's area they were confronted by a truly prodigious hunk of iron that Johnny and his assistants had begun to stoke up. Johnny explained this was his machine. He called it a locomotive or engine.

The Court was relieved to discover the machine would carry Johnny, not the other way around. They next inspected his burden and were unimpressed. It wasn't particularly heavy (except relative to the puny creature Johnny Eagle) though it was terribly un-wieldly, having two great arms, but, as they all cautioned Johnny, unwieldiness would not weigh in a pulling contest.

After the Court left for town B the preparations began in earnest. Everybody began to load up or har-ness up. Several individuals beat the starting gun and were away with their shouldered or wheeled loads. They were not the serious contenders, however, since all knew it would take a feat of considerable magnitude to win. Unless of course Johnny couldn't get started or his machine didn't work.

But Johnny could get started. He connected some cars to his engine and paused beside his burden which he called a crane. He put down skids and winched the whole thing onto a flatbed car and bolted it down. By the time he was ready to start out the roadway, both the town streets and the tracks Johnny's fellows had laid in the previous month were swarming with contestants more or less successful with their burdens. Some were staggering under great weights. Others were pushing or pulling with all their might, some resting every few yards and constituting obstructions. The lesser eleoxen contestants were cheered on by partisans largely because the three great hopes of the eleoxen couldn't get started. The team with the biggest load couldn't get it loaded. In fact it had been assembled on the spot and they couldn't even budge it. The team who could budge theirs succeeded in loading it on a mammoth wagon but didn't get ten paces before both axles cracked and broke. The third team, the largest of all, had great difficulty getting into harness and, not unexpectedly, all the gratuitous advice led to criticisms which led to blame which led to tempers which led to fights which, while terribly satisfying to the participants, left the complicated harness hopelessly tangled.

Johnny watched most of these efforts with amusement while waiting for the crowd of contestants who were getting away to thin. As a safety precaution he installed a triangular device in front that would nudge any eleoxen off the track if he proceeded gently.

The crowd along the roadway were treated to a real show. Here came Johnny Eagle rolling down the track with his big machine belching smoke and making such a racket. Spectators waved and he waved back. It was a brave sight.

When Johnny pulled into the destination town and up to the judges' stand he was actually the second to arrive. An eleoxen carrying a rather light burden who had set off before the starting gun had arrived first. When announcement of Johnny's victory was delayed and delayed it became apparent that the judges were wondering if they could get away with claiming a technical victory. As they went into a huddle once again Johnny gave instructions to his fellows and moved to the crane. When the lines were secured to the four corners of the judges' stand Johnny lifted the entire stand, startled judges and all, into the air and deposited them on the rearmost flatcar.

Before they could gather their wits to protest he reversed the train and began steaming slowly down the track while his fellows operating the crane began to swing aboard Johnny's eleoxen opponents, loads and all, from the adjacent roadway and dump them in the gondola cars located fore and aft of the crane car.

At first the fellows had to rig the slings or the lines to lift the eleoxen but as they progressed it became unnecessary. Spectators began to join in by tumbling or rigging the next contestant for transportation to the gondola cars. Soon even that was unnecessary as the farther toward the start the progression went the more

tired were the contestants. The struggling eleoxen would look ahead, see what was happening, roll their loads onto the sling and jump on top for the ride, only too willing to abandon the now obviously ended contest and join their fellows who seemed to be having great good fun.

It was for the judges a curious time. First they were startled, then interested in their ride, then possessed of a sense of fitness as they rode in state and dignity while those incompetent contestants were tumbled into the gondola cars to emerge grinning and waving. It was not until the curious phenomena which next occurred that they took occasion to pause and consider. As Johnny and his fellows proceeded down the track some of the homo spectators began to applaud. Soon those next in line began to applaud. Then those forward and backward began to applaud. It continued to flow forward and backward for ten miles of concentrated homos and the cumulative effect was thunderous. It was afterwards called Johnny's thunder. Natturally the judges did not like it one bit but it rose so unexpectedly and spontaneously that they could hardly hear each other let alone make themselves heard at the engine at the other end.

Naturally the next ruling council meeting was acrimonious. The eleoxen wanted to blame the snoxes but were in a bad way to do so for, as the Snox Chief said, not only did they lose but how in heavens name could they suffer themselves to submit to the unfortunate, indeed outrageous, lifting of slings and barrows and then proceed to ride like a bunch of children at a market fair.

There arose a general consensus that the whole thing had been a mistake and there were furtive glances cast at Eleoxen Six who had declined to participate in the seventh labor.

What was equally obvious was that the contests couldn't be called off. The public would not stand for it. This was clear even to the eleoxen faction though nothing else was. Sensing the upper hand, the snox faction moved with alacrity. We will save the day, they said, and when we have done so you shall acknowledge our superiority. We shall devise a strategy to result in the ultimate downfall of Johnny Eagle. Meanwhile the contests must continue as scheduled but they must be gradually wound down, not allowed to build up.

The eighth labor was an assignment to uncover the wealth of homosland. The subterranean homos dug in continuous effort for nearly the full cycle of a moon. They were driven first by their zeal to win; then, when gold wasn't where the snoxes said it would be, by their fear of failure.

Johnny meanwhile only observed the proceedings

and tinkered with his machines. That is, until disaster struck. The subterranean homos had penetrated deeper into the mountain than any prior homo ever had when part of their tunnel collapsed. Several snakehomos were rushed to the scene to see if they could penetrate the rubble and determine if there were any surviving miners. None returned. They were found subsequently when the mine was widened and shored and the surviving miners extracted.

This was accomplished under Johnny's direction and guidance by willing homos who, in a time of crisis, forgot all about sides. At least they forgot after the initial reaction which was ugly. Somehow, initially, many felt that the least Johnny could have done was to expose himself as had the brave miners; he hadn't done anything except talk to the miners coming off shift, marking his "charts" and taking walks.

Johnny ignored the growing rumble of menace, staked out a position on the other side of a ridge, and began to use a machine he called a drill. The menace subsided at the sight of Johnny and his fellows in turn feverishly at work. It evaporated completely when the drill broke through into the tunnel and it was found, against all hopes, that almost all of the miners were yet alive. Johnny drilled two more holes so the miners might get ventilation and sustenance while the rubble was cleared.

Meanwhile word had previously gone out in the corridors of bureaucracy to bring the guillotine and execute Johnny for failure. Unfortunately the guillotine and executioner arrived just as the mining community extracted their loved ones and were carrying Johnny Eagle around on their shoulders laughing and crying all the while.

Johnny was able to cancel not only his own beheading but also that of the executioner, the Chief Judge, and several other high ranking government figures nominated by the crowd of homos that closed ranks around him before the judges' stand.

But you failed, Johnny Eagle, whined the Chief Prosecutor.

No, I didn't, said Johnny. Ponder that.

In any case, the Chief Judge ruled, this labor had come to a non-jeopardy conclusion and, surrounding himself with bailiffs and marshalls, he scurried out of town to the next venue. Johnny was due there himself shortly but stayed for the evening's celebrations at the behest of the town.

For the ninth labor, the celebrants crowded around a lagoon near Coastal City. It was a festive day; the setting was idyllic; the sun bestowed its life-giving rays in just the right mixture of light and warmth to make the spectators conscious of neither. Such clouds as there were merely provided variety, not seriously impairing the view of the sunlit bottom of the deceptively deep clear lagoon.

The principal contestants were several fish homos and Johnny Eagle. Since the test was of the ability to be productive—in this case in water—all knew that the critical or telling contest would be between the whale-homo and Johnny Eagle. It was obvious that the challenge would be to see if Johnny, a land creature, could negotiate the water world.

None of those who arrived early were surprised to see Johnny's railroad pull onto the lagoon siding a huge machine that in fact was rather whale-like in appearance. What they were surprised to see was what appeared to be a monumental tub that the snoxes had constructed next to the lagoon.

The day progressed to everyone's delight, thanks to the antics of the porpoisehomos and their fellow smaller finny brethren. Expectation began to build when the whalehomo appeared in the mouth of the lagoon and circumnavigated it to the polite applause of the assembled homos (and Johnny, his mother, and his fellows).

The snox speaker who had emceed the program announced to all assembled that the contest had already begun, that Johnny's first challenge was to circle the lagoon. On water, not land, added the announcer. Every homo assumed that Johnny would be able to do that with his machine, undoubtedly a marine engine or locomotive. As they started to debate among themselves whether Johnny would pull the judges in the gondola cars the announcer announced that the whale would pull the judges around the lagoon in the wooden tub. The announcer called it a boat.

As the whale was being maneuvered into a harness and the tub launched, Johnny's crew launched his machine. To the disappointment of the snox strategists the machine didn't sink; why, heaven knows, for didn't the spy report it was made of metal. Johnny Eagle could not be trusted. Thank goodness they had arranged to steal his thunder. With great pomp and circumstance the judges entered the boat.

Johnny looked at Quen and predicted, There's going to be trouble.

At first awkwardly, and then with greater smoothness, the whale, boat, and Court began their tour of the lagoon. As the procession passed the assembled crowd applauded politely, dutifully, and maybe even apprehensively as they began to see that Johnny Eagle had been one-upped. The crowd began to shift its glances first from the boat to Johnny Eagle—he appeared unconcerned; then from Johnny to the boat—it was settling in the water as the procession progressed!

With a straight face Johnny told Quen: That's the trouble; they didn't put it in the water ahead of time to swell the wooden seams.

Or fill it with water while still on the bank, observed Johnny's chief engineer.

Soon it was no longer necessary to keep a straight face since as the Court progressed it became more and more apparent what was happening and the crowd began to titter. The judges assumed their most unconcerned, impartial miens as they gathered their robes. The titters turned to laughter and guffaws in direct proportion to the lifting of the robes and the lowering of the boat. In contrast the visages of the judges had gone from dignity to concern to panic.

It's time to go, said Johnny, motioning his crew aboard as the chief engineer slipped below. Johnny started the motor, engaged the screws, and began to follow the path taken by the whale, boat, court. True, he could have cut directly across the lagoon, but the boat, as Johnny knew was in no danger of sinking.

That was more than the Court knew as they began to shout for Johnny to hurry up. When Johnny pulled alongside they scrambled aboard and clung to the hull. As Johnny continued his circumnavigation of the lagoon one of the fellows (Johnny called him a steward) began to set chairs out in the deck area. The Court had to submit to a second tour as Johnny refused to put in to shore to off-load them.

Meanwhile, the poor whalehomo who had done all that was expected of him watched the progression from the center of the lagoon. He felt humiliated. It seemed that the jeers and catcalls were directed at him. He sounded and went to the very deepest part of the lagoon.

All could understand what had happened. They hadn't meant to poke fun at him; they immediately stopped but of course couldn't tell him. Even the judges understood; however to them it was simply irrelevant. They were in the process of issuing their umpteenth order to Johnny to return them to shore when the clever snox announcer claimed victory for homoskind. Suppose, he said, that a sunken treasure or something similar had been found. The whalehomo could be harnessed and bring it up. The judges took new heart.

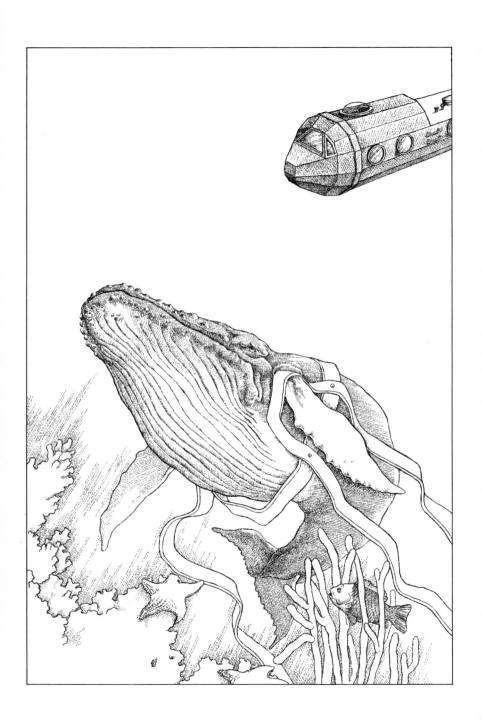

Johnny opened a hatch and told the judges that if they couldn't swim (none could) they had better get below since he was going to play Captain Nemo.

What's that? one judge asked.

Just a literary reference, said Johnny, as he closed the hatch and re-entered the conn.

The judges resisted and finally scrambled inside as it became obvious that the machine was sinking. It had been beyond their imagination that Johnny's machine was submersible. They flocked to the windows to view with awe the world from beneath the surface. They forgot themselves in their native excitement as they approached the bottom.

Johnny had steered his submersible toward the deepest part of the lagoon.

The crowd rushed to the bank. They could plainly see Johnny (or rather his machine) approaching the whalehomo.

This should do it, Johnny said to his chief engineer. Not even the biggest whalehomo could stomach those Jonahs in back. At first the judges were exhilarated at invading the domain of the whalehomo. Several pointed and laughed.

It was obvious that this deepened the chagrin of the whalehomo. He was very angry indeed. The judges sobered as they saw mayhem in his eye. All the crowd could see was that the whalehomo and Johnny Eagle were together.

There they were; eyeball to porthole.

Johnny winked.

Then he smiled.

They Approached the Bottom   123

The whalehomo stared . . . then he smiled. Then he winked, and with a flip of his giant flukes (to scare the judges) he turned, headed for the mouth of the lagoon, and was last seen headed in the direction of the Western Ocean.

A national emergency was declared before the 10th labor calling upon all homos to exert extra effort for the good of the family and to forego the 10th labor holiday unless directly involved. Since the labor was to take place in one of the most remote locales general attendance was in fact diminished.

The contest was between Johnny Eagle and the arts and crafts artisans of homosland. A wide variety of handicrafts were involved which were interesting both in end product and in fabrication. The fascination of Johnny, Quen and their fellows with the skills and abilities of the opposing contestants was exceeded only by the interest of the opposing contestants and their clan with the fabrication and ingenuity of Johnny and his machine for Johnny undertook to duplicate or approximate or create a utilitarian substitute for most of the products of the artisans with his magical substance— or at least that's what the artisans called it.

It was, at least so far as they were concerned, a magical substance for Johnny would take a blob of it, put it into his machine with a mold that his fellows had worked on, and create piece after piece of the appro-

priate design. It was the most marvelous stuff. It came out hard and shaped and was virtually impervious to heat and cold, to sun and water, and even to accidental breakage. The possible uses captured the imaginations of the artisans, and, besides that, the stuff was able to take on almost any color or, wonder of wonders, be left clear.

Such a spirit of fellowship and goodwill existed throughout the contest that if there seemed to be no winner then there also seemed to be no loser. The snox-eleoxen observers and judges tentatively challenged Johnny but felt themselves undercut when the arts and craft spokeshomo approached Johnny and asked if he would trade one of his machines with material and instructions for their crafts production for a year.

The eleventh labor of Johnny Eagle is the least understood, coming as it did between the voluntary restraint suggested as to attendance at the tenth labor and the absolute prohibition of attendance at the twelfth labor. It seems to have been a time of confusion.

The labor appears to have involved communication or transmittal of information. Apparently the snoxes used their secret corps of communicants. The test and results were either secret in nature or suppressed. Rough outlines, however, emerged from the obscurity.

Johnny apparently used, after repairs, the network of utility wires existing from pre-TV days to connect Capital City with the farthest inhabited frontier of the realm. Thereafter as a succession of snox couriers ran, flew, slithered, and swam from one terminus toward the other a battle of wits transpired.

The snoxes or, since they denied it, some other homo or group, arranged to disrupt Johnny's transmissions by the simple expedient of cutting the wires. The snoxes' satisfaction as Johnny's transmission was truncated after a few words turned to chagrin as it was resumed. It was soon stopped again and the two command posts became bustling centers each acting to a purpose as the race to complete or destroy ebbed and flowed.

The snox spy secreted near Johnny's strangely inactive machines conveyed all he overheard which at first was of some use as it involved words like wires, circuits, and relays but later were ineffective when Johnny, using words like beams, plasma, laser, and magrav, had obviously switched to a private code.

At the end an irate judge, forced to concede defeat, made the mistake of attacking Johnny Eagle and died mysteriously when Johnny applied "the force," as it was subsequently called by the snoxes.

Johnny related later that he had no choice, given the sabotage, but to use technologies beyond the capacities of homos to understand even though he had scrupulously avoided doing so heretofore. There is a certain crude justice, he observed, in that they forced me to resort to that form of transmission that transmits energy as well as information and thus put in my hand in extremis the instrument of my defense.

The Chief Judge and Snox Chief both sought to propitiate the very angry Johnny, explaining that the culprit judge was a weak-minded creature given to acting without thinking. They suggested that Johnny forgive and forget the experience.

Johnny coolly told them he had no intention of doing either and admonished them that until they understood that form—as the words forgive and forget—was connected to substance—those words' referrents—they would imperfectly understand both the moral and the material. Until homoskind identifies the non-contradictory, connected nature of these, it is destined to fail to deal successfully with either component, he sternly admonished.

The alarmed homo leaders held a council of war for the veneer of civility had been stripped from Johnny Eagle exposing him as a dangerous enemy of the state capable of using his powers against homoskind. That much was clear. What was less clear was what to do about it, for even the snox councilors could not say whether Johnny had exposed all of his powers when he had mysteriously zapped his attacker.

The younger eleoxen wanted to storm Johnny's school and eradicate the whole bunch with a frontal assault. The snox contingent suggested it would be stupid to attack him on his home ground since there he had virtually unlimited access to his machines, whereas, during the prior labors at least, he had only those connected with the task.

A spokeshomo for the young militants called the snoxes cowardly and observed that at least *some* homos were brave enough to face any enemy of homoskind. He became very belligerent when the Snox Chief tried to direct the discussion back to the problem and wouldn't sit down until he was told to go ahead and, by the way, did he have any idea where to attack. It seems, except that it was somewhere in The Polis, nobody knew for sure where to find Johnny Eagle. It was obvious even to the young eleoxen that if the hunter went charging around the hunted would vanish.

Then what must we do? the eleoxen asked.

It was at this point that the Grand Strategem of the snoxes was revealed, at first to the scepticism of the eleoxen and then to their grudging admiration.

The trial would continue. This would have the virtue of bringing Johnny and friends out in the open one last time. Unless somebody is rash and stupid enough to act hostilely toward them in the meantime, the Snox Chief admonished, glaring at the militant spokeshomo.

Secondly, it would have the virtue of showing the charity of homoskind by continuing in an evenhanded way in the face of gross provocation.

And, thirdly and principally, it would result in justice, actual and poetic, for the twelfth labor, the Chief announced, was: to fly. Johnny's last opponents were to be the Eagle Tribe. How fitting it was that the Eagle Tribe should be the downfall of Johnny Eagle. How fitting that soaring ambition should be brought to earth by, not hubris or jealous gods but, by a challenge to perform.

Homo is a flawed creature conceived in original sin and possessing a tragic nature, the Snox Chief lectured the young snoxes present. If it appears otherwise, the remedy is reductio ad sublimum. Push any outreaching fellow to the next level and he will outreach himself ultimately for in his pride he may be counted upon to overextend.

And, redirecting himself to the eleoxen, he continued, Johnny Eagle has overextended himself. As he has developed his coveted powers of reason he has become less and less homoslike until now he bears not even spiritual resemblance to his eagle ancestors. He is doomed to suffer the effects of his actions.

Let us have the twelfth labor, he stated sternly to the young militants and we shall be done with Johnny Eagle. If he survives any attempt to fly you may kill him. Frankly we expect him to try and to fail or crash. Johnny Eagle will eliminate himself.

Thanks to the preparation of the Chief Snox the crowd assembled for the twelfth labor had an edgy but satisfied mood. The public had been excluded and the attendees were confined to Johnny, Quen, their fellows from the school and numerous, but not quite all, representatives of homos officialdom. Virtually the entire government of homosland and their retainers were present that they might disseminate the result afterward.

None feared the size of Johnny's machine since in this instance at least it was apparent to all, even without snox explanation, that size was a negative. The bigger the machine the more certain the failure. When they arrived to find some of Johnny's fellows standing guard around a gigantic machine the observers breathed a sigh of relief. For while several young snoxes had given their all (died) in various attempts to emulate birds (with or without feathers applied) by leaping off cliffs to test various theories, there hadn't been time to test the lighter-than-air theory somebody came up with. Not to worry, they felt, as they gazed upon Johnny's machine parked before the judges' stand in a meadow outside The Polis.

And thus it was that matters came to a head. At a signal from the Chief Judge, Johnny moved to the dock preparatory to the start. Unbeknownst to him the same signal signalled the young militant eleoxen to move. They quickly and roughly rounded up Quen and all of Johnny's fellows and herded them into a pen directly across the meadow.

Jonny started, then, to the disappointment of those watching closely, turned his back on the hostages and asked the Snox Chief if he intended to bother allowing the trial to continue or if the incarceration of Quen and the fellows was the pre justice typical of non-rational mentalities.

The Chief Judge/Eleoxen, affronted by Johnny's addressing the question to another than himself, answered: The trial shall continue.

The Snox Chief who had assumed the role of

Prosecutor at this twelfth and last trial was not to be denied, however. He observed: Say what you will, Johnny Eagle, but do nothing or your fellows will die quick but painful deaths. Those young militants await only my signal or any untoward action on your part to act.

To the corporate disappointment of all who could hear, Johnny simply said: I understand.

The Snox Chief, goaded by this lack of perception of the situation, admonished: Make no mistake, this time you have overreached yourself. You cannot bluff your way through. Whatever your powers with other machines, at this moment you stand alone and neither you nor your fellows shall see the sun set this day in homosland.

Today you suffer the consequences of your misspent youth. You shall learn The Ultimate, that there is no individuality in death. You shall learn the emptiness and futility of reason—you who have not learned to propitiate the powers, omniscience and omnipotence. You who maintain words are the real world applied do not know how to speak the language of the snoxes or even of the eleoxen, the representatives of those powers on earth. You couldn't beg or intimidate, Johnny Eagle, if your life depended on it; and the irony is that it does. You are a dead man, Johnny Eagle.

We have disagreed about everything except one, the Snox Chief continued: the matter of life and death. We agree that the problem is life. You think it's for living.

And you don't, said Johnny.

It's more important than that, said the Snox Chief.

Nothing is more important or fundamental said Johnny. You threaten me with death ostensibly because you would punish me by taking away that which I value. Yet we both know it is more elemental than that. My continued existence is a threat to your continued existence. My continued existence would spell the end of homosland. You are striking out like the cowering cornered animal that you are.

You speak of irony but miss the best examples. Consider the irony of one man and his fellows cornering a culture it has taken generation upon generation to cultivate. Consider the irony that your culture is doomed if I stay and doomed if I go. Consider the irony that you who have powers that need propiation hold my mother and fellows hostage to my behavior.

You don't understand and therefore fear my power. You view it after your fashion, mystically. You strongly suspect I have what you have always sought—the unearned. *I don't*. There are only three powers or forces in the inhabited world: faith, force, and reason. All three are present today symbolically, existentially, and dynamically, and it is only the last, my power—reason—that rachets upward.

Do you know why there are no ordinary homos present today? It is not because they might see the effect or consequence of reason, but that they might see the consequence of faith and force. As long as you presented to the world only faith and force there wasn't much to choose between. It was one master or the other or both together.

In truth you are less fearful of their seeing the power of reason than the bankruptcy of faith and force. They might at long last comprehend the difference between wealth created and earned through reason applied and wealth mooched and looted. You sit there in your cloth of gold perpetuating the great historical fraud that homo must choose between faith and force. You have suppressed for centuries at a time the truth that the choice is to think or not to think. Only in the latter case does the choice become faith or force and frankly that's a choice between tweedledum and tweedledee.

You who have dedicated your life to the principle that life is not what life is about find homo all too willing to agree that the incomprehensible is hopeless. As the parties established, you have perpetuated your rule with minor variants for an unreasonable period of time and for this, if blame were placed, every single homo who chose, consciously or not, not to think is at fault.

All homos are created equal. There are no instincts and no innate knowledge. All that a creature is he becomes—after birth. The things that happen to him and that he does determine what he is and will become. Physical appearance, color, and wealth are irrelevant except as they might impede or accelerate exposure to reason. I was fortunate in that I was not burdened by non-rational parents nor by a non-rational education, but had I been it still would have been my task individually to become rational.

Johnny paused, then continued. Every creature is born a man but he must grow up to be one. I am.

135

When the time comes I shall die like one but for now that doesn't interest me much. I am more interested in living like one.

Brave talk, Johnny Eagle, snarled the Prosecutor. Look over there toward the horizon. Those two approaching creatures are eagles—proper eagles. As they approach you would do well to consider your demise. You are separated from your fellows. You shall receive neither support nor solace. Those two eagles, aged as they are, shall be your downfall as they were your father's, for they were the carriers of your father at his death. It is most fitting that they should be present at yours. When they arrive your course is run, Johnny Eagle: if homos had been meant to fly he would have feathers. If you turn your back on nature, be prepared to suffer the penalty. You cannot do the impossible, he stated.

Can you? asked the Chief Judge.

No, said Johnny Eagle. I cannot do the impossible; no one can.

The Chief Judge looked relieved, then smug, then righteous.

Nor have I any intentions of turning my back on nature, Johnny continued, as he watched the eagles land on stanchions located on two forward corners of the judges' stand. Turning his back to the Prosecutor he addressed the Chief Judge: Is this a debating society or a trial by ordeal?

The Chief Judge who had followed little of the dialogue found this easy to handle.

A trial by ordeal, he responded.

Then, let's get on with it, said Johnny with what the young eleoxen recognized as great bravado.

I propose, said Johnny, to fly through the air like an eagle, to circle the mountain on the western horizon and return. Further, I propose to carry with me the Court, the Prosecutor, and the principal governmental officials of homosland.

The Chief Judge, remembering his trip to the bottom of the lagoon, brightened perceptibly until he heard the Snox Chief warn: No, No, it's a trick. He would be satisfied to kill not only himself but the elite of homosland in a last desperate gesture.

The Chief Judge/Eleoxen, much shaken by this near-fatal adventure, was wrathfully disposed toward Johnny Eagle. He heartfeltly thanked the Snox Chief for his advice and asked him for recommendations.

The Snox Chief, struck with an inspiration, saw a way to nail Johnny and his entire tribe without martyrdom. He suggested loading the hostages in the heavier-than-air craft if Johnny meant to run his bluff and continue.

Whereupon Johnny became very exercised: No, No, Brer Snox, not the airplane.

That was enough for the Chief Judge. He ordered Johnny and the hostages aboard the machine.

As the hostages were marched aboard the machine Johnny was informed that all of the possessions of the man tribe were forfeit and subject to confiscation wherever found.

This didn't upset Johnny so the Snox Chief continued: Further, we have confiscated all of the machines you have previously left with your opposing contestants.

At that information Johnny did react, but he appeared saddened, not angry. It will do you no good, he told the Snox Chief, and for most it will cut the last link to the world as a rational, controllable place, a place of expectations limited only by the power to perceive them.

You may have the machines, he continued, but you do not have the key to use them.

The Chief Eleoxen interrupted with a smirk: The snoxes thought of that. We've looked. There are no keyholes.

Johnny looked at the Snox Chief. Your machinations have succeeded. You sought justice; you will get justice. The irony of the situation is that justice doesn't have to be sought. It can't be evaded. Your pursuit of it in the general and the particular was nothing but the attempt to evade consequences. You say there is no cause and effect; let me tell you, there is. I was told, Check your premises, Johnny Eagle. Let me add to that: Check your consequences.

In the particular and immediate, you shall collect the reward of Snox Law. Snox Law is Gresham's Law applied to the intellect. How long do you think you will survive without your enemy, the rational mind, present to feed upon. Only in my case the body, having been reunited with the mind, does not intend to serve as a corporeal host. Possessing intention, my body will act in a pro-life, not a sacrificial, manner. Just as a cancer dies when the body it saps dies, so, you will find, will you, individually and collectively.

In the general and long run, the death sentence you pronounce today is on yourselves and your heirs.

In the long run, the Chief Judge interposed, we are all dead.

"In the long run we are all dead." That is one of life's major philosophic statements, Johnny mused. It sums up the essence of selflessness. Tomorrow will take care of itself; conduct has no consequences, cause no effect; posterity is its own problem.

It is the selfish who think otherwise. It is the selfish who consider posterity their problem today. It is the selfish who so conduct themselves that the consequences of their actions leave a better world for their children and their children's children because it pleases them to do so. It is the selfish who provide, not only materially but spiritually, for tomorrow. It is the selfish who care about themselves in the abstract—about themselves as man—as creatures possessing a quantity and quality of life that distinguishes them from sub-human existence. Man the rational, sapient, selfish creature acts to perpetuate his species. That he does so does not distinguish him from the lowest animal form. That he does so by reason distinguishes him as the highest animal form. In this he and he alone must make decisions of life or death, of mortality—of morality. Instincts, reflexes, or vibrations are non-decisional, non-rational. Choice and volition create morality, not the other way around.

The statement of the most moral, the most rational man, the most selfish man, would be: In the long run man will live. And such a man would act accordingly. It is the selfish man, the moral man, who cares. It is the selfish who is man.

The power that you have connived to defeat was too simple for your poisonous minds to understand and too noble for your machiavellian bent to practice.

We, each of us, the rational and the irrational, get what we deserve. That is the justice you sought to evade in your pursuit of justice.

Do you know what will happen next? I will tell you. You shall reap what you have sown. Truisms have served countless generations and survived; ask yourself why. They are genuine philosophical remarks rendered in the vernacular. Causes have their effects— premises their consequences. You have sown the seeds of faith and force and you shall reap the consequences. The consequences shall be effects consistent with the absence of reason. Some of you shall experience the effects of anti-reason; some of non-reason. Until someone—some one person—decides to think, to initiate the process of self-sustaining spontaneous generation, your world will eclipse into darkness and ultimately, from your standpoint, into void.

Johnny, having kept an eye on the loading of his plane, turned and walked up the ramp to the door. As he entered he turned and looked back at the assembled crowd.

A voice, hesitantly brave, then committed, said, Wait! Wait, Johnny Eagle!

Johnny looked. All of the snoxes and eleoxen looked, but the questioner went on.

At your trial by words you identified the key concepts, life, reason, and justice. Today you spoke of them again. Before you go, are there any more key words? Or concepts? he added.

Johnny looked long and hard at the young snox who had been so brash as to ask that question. That look and the smile that followed obliterated all of the censorious vibrations the young snox had felt. Johnny spoke the last two words:

Freedom and Happiness.

Then he entered the machine, climbed to the cockpit, and started the engines. The noise no longer scared the homos. That the machine was steerable no longer occasioned surprise. When the machine had rolled the length of the field confidence rose in the hearts of most.

He's failed, they began to say. Then the machine turned into the wind and began to pick up speed.

The assembled judges, governmental officials and other functionaries watched as the machine rolled faster and faster down the pasture. They watched in awe as it lifted off the ground. Each knew that momentarily it would crash in flames. They watched and waited, and waited and watched. Their unease grew in relation to the distance and time of Johnny's flight.

The last seen of Johnny Eagle and his followers was the speck of the flying machine disappearing into the sunset over the top of the distant mountain. Then they listened and listened for the sound of a crash. They didn't hear it.

Consternation.

It must have crashed, said one. Yes, said another, too far away to hear. It had to, said another; it was impossible. It didn't happen, said another. Right, we have been fooled, said another. Mass hypnosis, said some. There never was a plane, said several. There never was a Johnny Eagle, said most.

Wait. We hear it. Everybody listened intently.

He said he would circle over the far mountain and return, reminded a snox.

They looked.

No, he said if we were on board he would circle and return, said Eleoxen 27. He never said he would return with our hostages.

Recriminations.

We have been tricked, said the Chief Eleoxen. It's all your fault, he said to the Snox Chief.

No, it is your fault, said the Snox Chief.

It is both of your faults, said Eleoxen Six. This is what happens when weaklings rule. Whereupon he slew the Chief Eleoxen and the Snox Chief.

Pandemonium.

Part The Third

. . . AND CONSEQUENCES

Chapter VI

IN THE ENDING

WHAT HAPPENED NEXT? asked the littlest turtle.

It was almost as if Johnny's last remarks had been a prophecy or a curse, replied the elderly turtle.

Even though no one but the Council and most members of the government had watched the last labor, somehow everybody knew what had happened. But nobody knew what to do or what it meant.

The snox contingent spread throughout the land proclaiming that the twelfth labor had no meaning. Nothing had meaning, so why worry.

They were not noticeably successful in restoring tranquility to an increasingly uneasy land.

Neither were the eleoxen homos, though they administered a greater and greater quantity of justice from one moon to the next with their guillotine. Eleoxen Six sulked. The eleoxen at large became so busy, in fact, that trial and judgment was turned over completely to the snoxes.

It seemed that everyone was restless. In Farmregion, the homos with a carnivore ancestry petitioned to be allowed to eat meat. The lionhomos and their fellows presented what they thought was a very good case, but the snoxes ruled against them. The carnivore homos were very upset. When their motion for new trial was overruled, they ate the judges.

The rest of the homos appealed to the eleoxen for protection. The eleoxen didn't know what to do except for E-6, who laughed. They finally compromised: the snoxes would explain why the carnivores were right to do what they did, and the eleoxen would contain the carnivores in one section of the country, the section they were in. Since this suited the carnivores' purpose, at least for the moment, an uneasy peace was established.

If anyone asked about the non-carnivore homos in Carnivoreregion, they were told by the snoxes that it was a divine punishment for lack of faith. It was, in fact, a divine visitation by The Ultimate upon those agrarian homos who dared to believe that the antiultimate (not "Johnny Eagle," they were prohibited to say his name) had not only been right but had even ever been.

Johnny Eagle, said the snoxes, had never existed. (Somehow nobody asked how *they* could say his name.) The proof was the trials and tribulations of the agrarian homos who had been the first (not as a group, but individually) to believe in Johnny Eagle.

Not immediately, but soon the second of the homo regions to fall was the Capital. No, not because it was the seat of government, but because it was the seat of business. Everything was falling to pieces. The food-stocks that had been adequate when the agrarian homos had worked their long days were no longer there. That was understandable—those who hadn't been eaten stayed indoors to keep from being eaten.

What nobody had foreseen was that the drayage homos had nothing for their wagons to pull from farm to market. The market homos had nothing to sell to purchasers who, because the manufactories couldn't operate without healthy homos, soon had nothing to buy it with anyway. For a long time everybody made do with what they had which was less and less.

Soon bands of homos began to range the land—at first taking the possessions of their wealthier brethren, and then taking their lives and bodies as well. As the land lay underdeveloped, soon everything became wild again. It was a time when the law of the wild—that the strongest shall prevail—came into being.

As a result of this state of affairs, four groups began to form. The largest was the main body of homos who didn't know what to do.

What to do? they asked, and scared themselves by the question.

Bring back Johnny Eagle, said the second group. His strength was of the mind. He didn't hurt anybody, he helped. The stronger he got, the fairer he became, peeped one frail little creature, looking over his shoulder.

This sort of talk seemed to spring up everywhere and aroused the remaining two groups which were the successors to the snox and eleoxen groups that had fallen into disarray after the departure of Johnny Eagle.

E-6 had gone off in a sulk because his actions weren't understood. The rest of the eleoxen wandered about either trying to get a snox to tell them what to do or doing what came naturally by bullying any ordinary homo who came within their reach. On the other hand, the snox community had endless conclaves and meetings. There seemed to be a lack of leadership since no one could form a consensus that any other snox should become Snox-1.

Actually some of the snox and eleoxen factions were secretly pleased since the confusion allowed them to establish their own areas of influence. In effect, they became rulers and councilors of mini-domains. This in fact started bringing order out of the chaos because life became more understandable. Through the power of the eleoxen groupings and the statecraft of the snox groupings, the mini-domains were taken over one by one by one group or the other until there existed several roughly equal sections that didn't necessarily bear any relation to the old suburbities.

One of the oldest snoxes said it could be called a group of nations. One of the youngest snoxes said it was the natural development of society since the several nations represented a balance of power. It might be, the homos felt to themselves; certainly further progress had been made in animalification. Each subspecies seemed to be making great strides toward the logical extension of their way of life. If the turtles and cranes seemed to be behind, well, they were notoriously long-lived creatures, and their generations would not have progressed very far. Consider the rabbithomos: hardly anybody called them anything but rabbits anymore. It was even rumored that the chickenhomos in some nation had succeeded in laying eggs rather than giving birth to live childhomos.

A substantial number of homos had begun not to be disquieted anymore. Somehow it wasn't that things weren't right; they weren't wrong either. No, that wasn't it. It was not a matter of right or wrong.

Things were. What's wrong with that? was a question they had dislearned, except perhaps for the Eagle-lists, which those few who wanted to search for and bring back Johnny Eagle were called.

It was this latter group of conservative reformers, a small, well-meaning, semi-knowledgeable group who, if they weren't the cause of, were at least the occasion for the counter-reformation. However long the conservatives talked about the past and how good in the name of justice things had been, somehow most homos understood that they were a fringe group. As far away as things were from the conservatives' justice somehow the bulk of homoskind, while acknowledging their points, still dimly knew in their hearts that the answer to life, if there was one, was not to be found backward.

Throwback Homos (Reformers)
Conservative (Male) and More Liberal (Female)

The conservatives, however, did serve as the focal
point of the new tirades of E-6, for E-6 seemed to
awaken as from a hibernation during which the homos
had tried as best they could to sort themselves out. Actually, some opined that it was S-9 who had re-
awakened E-6. It was thought to result from the battle
for supremacy that followed the deaths of E-1 and S-1.

There was, you see, sort of an interregnum after those deaths when the E's and the S's were disorganized. Actually, the two groups had widely different problems.

As to the E's, nominally there was no problem, for E-2, E-3, E-4 and E-5 survived and most of the other E's looked up to them to give E-6 his due. Unfortunately, the view from the top down wasn't quite the same. Neither E-2, E-3, E-4 nor E-5, nor all of them together, was willing or apparently able to give E-6 his due. Let sleeping E-6's lie, they said to one another. With a lack of leadership there was a noticeable lack of followership.

As to the S's, the opposite problem was true. Since S-ness was based on self-abnegation, charity and altruism, the professed equality of all who weren't S-1 necessitated the position that anyone who wasn't S-1 was the equal of every other, even the humblest. As a result, when there wasn't an S-1, almost everybody (except the humblest) offered himself for the position. Naturally the greatest acrimony was to be found in the claims of S-2, S-3, S-4, etc., in descending order. The exception was S-9 who kept his counsel and observed the others. When none of the factions sought to offer him as a compromise he observed further and finally called a meeting of S-homos. He will announce his candidacy, said the skeptical S-2 through S-8. Even so, they came to the meeting because all the rest of the S-homos were coming. (After all, who wouldn't when it was rumored bread and wine were to be passed out?)

153

After food and drink for all, S-9 arose and declared to the throng that he was not a candidate for S-1. S-1 was a saint, he declared, and proceeded to eulogize S-1 in terms common to their breed. The longer he went on, the more blatant appeared the self-serving acts of S-9's nominal superiors. S-9 concluded that no one could replace S-1, least of all himself. The S-homos were greatly moved. He is right, was the general consensus. How could we not see it? How base of us to aspire, said others. S-9 is surely a fine S-homo, they generally agreed. Surely he is first amongst us, they murmured to each other. S-9 shall be S-1, they began to shout.

No, no, cried SS 2-8. He and his henchmen who are pouring wine are spreading those thoughts amongst you.

How unworthy, the S-homos cried. S-9 shall be invested S-1 on the morrow's eve.

Seeing they could get nowhere with the increasingly boisterous crowd, SS 2-8 agreed to adjourn to the next evening.

When all assembled the next night, the S 2-8 group had their counter-strategy planned and their henchmen scattered among the crowd.

Bring S-9, the crowd cried. Here he comes, could be heard.

And indeed here came S-9 in stride with E-6 and a procession of E's in his train. As he mounted the rostrum, the E's spread out around the perimeter of the S's. S-homos began to glance at one another and shift nervously.

S-9 began, My fellow homos, I bring you good news. In the name of our revered leader, who preached love, especially to one's enemies, I have reconciled ourselves with the E's. You are met to proclaim me S-1, but hear now that I again put off that mantle. Hear rather that henceforth there shall be no S-1 or E-1. At the stirrings of the S's and incipient grumblings of SS 2-8 and their henchmen the E's came to attention and tightened the perimeter. The mutterings subsided. My fellow homos, proclaimed S-9, from this day hence, you shall live in an era of love. He went on to outline the effect of reconciliation with the E's. It shall be as it was before, he enthused, or even better. Indeed, it shall be a golden era. His enthusiasm was infectious not only among the S's but among the E's too, except for E-6, who stood and watched.

In the spirit of universal brotherhood we shall dispense with S's and E's as names and take as appropriate to our species, the name "deos," which in our prestory days meant gods, for are we not jointly the most powerful of all species?

All agreed readily, and the name was accepted by acclamation. If the ex-E's were less vocal in doing so, it was not that they were reluctant, but that unlike the slippery tongued ex-S's, they had trouble getting their thick tongues to articulate diphthongs.

But what of the rest of homoskind? asked one deos (an ex-S, since even though E's had the prerogative to question the practice had largely fallen into disuse).

We shall love them as our children, was the response.

155

Are they also to be called deos?

No, as children they cannot be expected to possess the qualities of their . . . he sought for a word . . . older equals.

Yes, that is clear, they replied. How are you to be addressed? they asked. Are you Deo One? the questioner asked, and hastily added, Is E-6 Deo One, too?

Deo One (ex-E-6) had to club down one dimwitted associate who insisted they had been insulted. It was agreed that there would be no numbers in this equal world and all should be addressed as plain deos, or citizen deos or comrade deos.

Cause proclamations to spread throughout the land, decreed Deo One (ex-S-9). We have stopped the breakdown of society. A new era is dawning. Manifestly, we must bring the kingdom back together, said Deo One to Deo One. You, Deo One (ex-E-6), and your deos shall spread throughout the land and bring equality and education to the homos. Meanwhile, we shall seek enlightment through communion with the mother of us all, Nature, proclaimed Deo One.

Agreed, said Deo One.

For the next several years the deos spread through the land bringing equality and education to the homos. It was a large and arduous task, but they were equal to the work.

Unfortunately, due to bad communications and

thick tongues, homokind misheard the name of their educators and could be heard to run through the streets calling: The dinos are coming, the dinos are coming. The dinos [ex-deos (ex-E's, ex-eleoxen)] didn't object. First of all, what's in a word? Secondly, the dinos couldn't say it better anyway. And thirdly, they never were at ease with the same name as those puny deoses (ex-S's, ex-snoxes).

In point of fact, the dinos had in the intervening years grown very large and powerful as they brought education to the masses. They had to be reminded by their group leaders that the occasional hermit or pilgrim deo they saw was their equal and was to be treated with respect. The truth was they had more respect for the masses. For while the common homo more or less persevered, the deos were seen physically to wane, not wax as had the practical dinos.

This was, of course, explained by Deo in his teachings as a sign of the prospering of the spiritual side of that pitiful, sinful creature homos. "As the flesh wanes the soul waxes," uttered Deo. This unearthly wisdom was so profound that the rest of the deos took it up as a chant. Not surprisingly, it brought great solace and peace to their lives. No more did they quake in the presence of a dino lest the unholy creature forget their (the deos') place.

In the early years when some lowly, humble deo was set upon and killed by the brutish dino it was occasion for sorrow and ceremony. Each death was taken to be a demonstration of the superiority of the deos faith over matter.

Most of the early casualties occurred among the pilgrims and hermits of the outreaches. Deo had explained their virtue to his flock. They are saints, he said. They shall be venerated and a day set aside to their memory.

How righteous, said they all, more and more in awe of the teachings of Deo.

The deos society was seen to have diminished as many of their numbers set out for pilgrimage and to become hermits. As the years passed, there came to be an increasing number of saints. They finally came so rapidly that they ran out of days. What shall we do? said the high deos, who had come to wait upon Deo day and night lest some inspired word leak from his communication with the Cosmos.

No answer was forthcoming. How profound, they told their lesser colleagues. Strive and apply yourselves in the hope you too shall some day achieve such wisdom. He is withdrawn into the fullness of The Ultimate, explained the high deos. He is perfection on earth, the living symbol of things spiritual, they explained. Meanwhile, the problem of ever increasing saints was mounting. At first, they named two saints for every day, but since that was not well received, the high deos decided to not question but communicate with Deo, whereupon on an appointed day, with great ceremony, they retreated to the humble shack where Deo had last seated himself in the lotus position. When they emerged days later, emaciated and stumbling, but glowing with what they could only describe as a mind expanding experience full of lights and sights and

shapes and sounds and, most importantly, with revealed appreciation, they announced that they had the
answer to the problem of saints: the year would be ex-
panded.

Of course, said the acolytes.

But! countered the high deos, that does not mean
every application is to be honored. There shall be a
rigorous examination concerning any candidate for
sainthood, for you must see that it is an honor ac-
corded only to the most worthy.

After several years (nobody had thought to count
the moons) there came upon the deos considerable
concern about Deo, who, while he had given several
revelations, had not been seen to eat or drink anything
for the longest time nor to have spoken directly to
either the greatest or the least of his disciples.

A considerable debate arose which gave rise to the
possibility of schisms which all agreed were untenable.
Accordingly, the high deos fasted forty days and forty
nights in the presence of Deo. The doors of the shrine
(for so it had come to be called when the young deos
would slip surreptiously before it and kneel in prayer)
were thrown open before the assembled deos.

On the fortieth day, the Chief High Deo approached DEO, all prior efforts to elicit direct communication having failed, and touched HIM on the shoulder. On the instant of the touch, DEO crumbled into

dust. The Chief High Deo was seen to reel back and collapse in the midst of his peers.

Awe. Thrashing and Renting. Prayers and Supplications. Arguments.

A minority held that the Chief High Priest had profaned the person of the DEO, who was too sacred to touch. They left the compound to go out into the world when they were scoffed at by the majority, who held that the Chief High Priest was but the instrument of DEO, who had reached The Ultimate: that state of being that transcended flesh and blood and had become pure spirit. It was universally held that a miracle had occurred and that DEO's chosen band had witnessed it.

Clearly this miracle was Sainthood carried . . . to . . . to . . . to the miraculous. Numerous were the instances of trial and tribulation of the flesh at the hands of the dinos but never before, they realized, had a humble homo done it to himself. This was The Ultimate. Now they had a name for it and its name was DEO.

Deep overcoming emotion swept the assembly.

Unfortunately, the dense dinos could not be made to comprehend the significance of what had happened. Never, lamented the Most Venerable Chief High Deo, has the gulf between the deos and the dinos been wider, but, he added, in the wisdom of DEO, you must understand that this is proper.

Fortunately he warned his community that an era of trial and tribulation lay ahead of them, a time of testing of their faith and worthiness. Fortunately it was, for so it transpired.

While it had been relatively peaceful for the deos when the dinos were roaming the countryside, bringing peace to the land, it was not when the dinos began quarreling among themselves. They were always prone to do so but at first Deo/Dino One had only to indicate his displeasure. Later, he did so at the dino unification meeting and he was challenged by several representatives of the governed territories. It was agreed that all couldn't fight one, so they would fight each other, the survivor to rule.

A particularly ferocious dino, Tyranos by name, who was neither the biggest nor the fleetest nor the cleverest, won, and proclaimed himself King.

Well, said the turtle, there began a long period in our history when Tyranos' clan roamed abroad in the land. They killed and destroyed at whim. Most of the homos appealed to the deos to do something. Whereupon the Most Venerable Chief High Deo admonished them that it was all their fault for not being properly worshipful of DEO and respectful of the deos. They stoned him for his stupidity, and yet why not hedge their bets, they argued. So accordingly they gathered all of the High Deos together and sent them to appeal collectively to their King, Tyranos. When King Tyranos tired of hearing the deos' petitions and then their supplications and then their prayers, he heard their cries.

It was said by the remnants of the deohomos that there were more saints created that day than any other. The remaining deos scattered. Everybody scattered. Society scattered.

A
Particularly
Ferocious
Dino

It came to pass that the ferocity of the tyranos homos was so developed that they turned on themselves and, in what afterwards was viewed as a short period of time, fought each other to the end.

The Rage of the Tyranos

How did the homos protect themselves during the rage of the tyranos? asked the littlest turtle.

Most of them didn't. Some who could took to the air or the sea, said the old turtle. The majority of the rest took refuge in caves. It is from the last group that we have inherited most of the indirect knowledge of Johnny Eagle, he added. They were very conservative in their thought and habit. They called themselves the keepers of the past and believed the answers to all problems were to be found there.

They had certain shibboleths, chief among which was the word "freedom." Possibly due to the large number of deohomos who took refuge in their midst at the time of the deos dispersion, they attached mystical significance to the word and anything they determined was associated with it. These troglatives, as they were called, wished to force prayer into education in the name of freedom; their chief spokeshomos supported suspension of rights in the name of right (but to be fair, only in times of national emergency); and they were against abortion in the name of freedom. Freedom didn't seem to be of choice, because that presupposed rationality which had long been discarded, but rather for what they called the soul which didn't require rationality and attached *in utero.*

It was always a matter of bewilderment to these troglatives that the rest of the creatures couldn't see such things and flock to their banners. They were forced to conclude that they had special ability to perceive beyond that of the common creature; but, they were very generous with their desire to help everybody else perceive the right.

And was that the end of the devolution of homoskind? asked the littlest turtle.

No, that came with the successors to the troglatives. They were a group who were much more liberal. They criticized their predecessors, not for their special ability to perceive the truth (which in fact, they had to admit, they themselves had inherited) but for errors of application. Freedom meant total freedom, they said. As long as no creature infringed upon another, any creature of any persuasion was to be admitted to their temple, for they built a great temple that reached almost to the sky.

On top of the temple, they proposed to erect a totem spelling FREEDOM in giant letters. Unfortunately, when they placed the last great letter atop their great tower, the whole thing collapsed. No one is quite sure why, but, while they were possibly the most vocal of homos, their words lost connection with reality. Thereafter any animal could associate with the babeltarians provided only that he professed to worship the totem freedom.

Chapter VII

SITNALTA

YES, YES, THAT BRINGS us to the present, said the littlest turtle, but what of Johnny Eagle? He's not of the present, is he?

No creature knows, said the old turtle, for though a legend exists and seems to grow from time to time, it may be just a myth built around the initial events. One aspect of the legend is that Johnny Eagle returns from time to time to collect artifacts left behind or to collect creatures he chooses, but nobody knows.

The last anyone saw of Johnny Eagle was when he stepped aboard the flying machine and flew off over the mountains into the setting sun. Yes, it's rumored he did land, said the old turtle, anticipating the littlest turtle's next question. The legend has it that he and his band landed on a vast continent that rose from the Western Ocean to receive them. This land was called Sitnalta, and it was here that Johnny, Quen and their fellow students set foot on a new world to create anew the race of creatures called MAN.

What do we know of them? asked the littlest turtle.

Legend has it that they are a diverse sort with no attention paid to size, shape or color—only to the fundamental, that they be sapient. We know nothing directly, but we may make some guesses, said the old turtle. The troglatives had a great campaign to recapture Johnny Eagle and bring him back. They instituted a world search for Johnny or Sitnalta. I, myself, have made several journey-searches in my lifetime, said the turtle, but nothing has been found of Johnny Eagle except for the artifacts, remnants and fragments of his life in homosland prior to his departure.

His old school was found by the snoxes several years after his trial, but the material found was either fragmentary or, as many suspected, destroyed by the deohomos during their reign. It was rumored that they considered the remnants evil and heretical. The troglatives later rediscovered the temple of Johnny Eagle. At first they thought he had made sacrifical offerings in his temple, called a library, but it was later determined that the deohomos had burned the contents, called books, one by one.

Did anything survive? interjected the littlest turtle.

Yes, there were several things: in one place a statue of Johnny Eagle; in another a statue of Johnny's mother; some few books were scattered about; and, several things called writings or manuscripts that the oldest scholars of our society, called scribes, as were all their ancestors, could not read since in the memory of the oldest scribe no one had written. Even books were considered an arcane hobby of doting old creatures.

What did the writings say? Can we see the statues? Where are these things? When . . .

The old turtle interrupted the littlest turtle's rush of questions. You may know all there is to know if you wish, for you children are possibly among the last to search for Johnny Eagle. For generations we turtles have traveled the earth to find Johnny Eagle. This is your assigned task in life, he said. Your journey begins with my narrative.

You may inspect the artifacts as is your prerogative as journey-searchers, but don't be disappointed. There are no maps or other hints that any of us have found, he said. Occasionally we used to come upon other turtle creatures at the outreaches of our travels, but those turtles could tell us nothing. Either they were remnants of the old order or had progressed further than we had.

Of the little turtle auditors, almost two out of three opted out of continued investigation. In this they were supported by many of their parents who believed their prowess as explorers was built on the playing fields.

The first sight the remaining little turtles saw was the statue of Quen, Johnny's mother. It had probably been disfigured by the deohomos. Most thought it interesting in a disquieting way. Some dropped out and rejoined their fellows when they discovered that, contrary to their expectations, the statue was much smaller than the statue they had seen of King Tyranos.

When the scribe homos exhibited the books and writings, the turtle auditors began dropping out by two's and three's until only the littlest turtle and a little

Quen Eagle

girl turtle were left. The littlest turtle communicated his interest and excitement to her and was rewarded in turn by her admiration of his interest. This was important to him because absolutely everyone else teased him. They teased her too, but she had learned too much to be dissuaded. Their interest fed each other. The smart get smarter, said the littlest turtle, mixing the aphorisms he was learning while learning to translate from the books into oral language. If only anyone knew the secret of writing, sighed the littlest turtle, looking at the quantity of writings that remained as against the few books that hadn't been burned.

The two little turtles spent several moons continuing their search, sometimes with the scribes and sometimes with the books, and sometimes only with each other, talking. Nobody cared because the littlest turtle was a runt of no promise, and the girl was, well, a girl. The few friends they had seldom came around. The littlest turtle thought it was because they didn't have the same interests, but the others confided to their friends that the runt was growing uglier every time they saw him.

One day the old turtle, now even more aged and decrepit, came to visit. They chatted a short while and an extraordinary thing happened. The old turtle asked if the littlest turtle had discovered anything about Sitnalta or Johnny Eagle. Before he answered the littlest

171

turtle thought furiously. What was wrong? Then he identified it. The old turtle had asked him a question. Never in his experience had an adult ever asked a child a question. As soon as he perceived this, he became flustered and embarrassed, but with the patience of the old turtle and the support of the little girl turtle, he proceeded to tell of the little they had discovered.

Sitnalta, he began, will be a land peopled by men—creatures of reason. Their primary means of confronting life—of living—will be solving problems through the application of their minds. Reason will be their means of survival. Although the work of Johnny Eagle at his labors suggests that the application of the mind brings consequences of such a radical nature that life may not be experienced in a rational society as a matter of survival, but rather as a matter of enjoyment, I think it is important to emphasize man's means of survival lest in a time of plenty he lose track of his basic nature.

These creatures, if they exist, called man, will be problem-solvers. If a problem arises, they will solve it; it is as simple as that. Conceivably some problems would take longer or shorter amounts of time to solve, but in the end they must all be solved—unless man should suspend his power, reason. For some reason I can't figure out his, our, ancestors seem periodically to have done so.

Specifically what such a society would look like is almost beyond my imagination. Assuming a dedication to reason, one would have to know sequentially what series of problems had been confronted, for one problem breeds another. For instance, Johnny went from motorcycle to train to boat to airplane. What happened next? How do people of Sitnalta transport themselves and their goods? I can't guess, though I would dearly love to know. I do know this much: if living doesn't present them with enough problems, the most rational wouldn't be happy unless they could invent problems for themselves.

The Old Turtle paid many visits to LT and LGT, as he called them. The visits came to be looked forward to by both the teacher/student and the students/teachers.

As far as I can make out from the books, man (or perhaps he wasn't really man at those times, mused LT) had come to believe that happiness was some sort of euphoric, unreal, mindless feeling which was the end to life. This seems to have had considerable consequences. Being contrary to his nature, it was only realized momentarily by certain drug users who succeeded in overwhelming that nature. On the other hand, such mindlessness, being unreal, became the special province of the supranatural, of those we would call deohomos of one variety or another. The biggest problem, however, was for the truly manly man who couldn't reconcile the irreconcilable. When he had problems, instead of viewing them as opportunities, he was told they were a curse, an original sin, a part of his nature. He tore himself apart trying to be a contradiction. It is no wonder that they created the idea anxiety to describe the irreconcilable: life and the irrational.

We have a book, said LGT, that says man at his most glorious used only 25% of his brain. Can you imagine what it would be like if he used the other 75% or even another 25%? she asked. While we suspect this is more a matter of quality than quantity, we can't imagine what proper use of reason would bring, so we can't tell you what Sitnalta looks like. It must be—no, not glorious—say rather exciting, interesting, and challenging.

Johnny Eagle seems to have made similar observations, said LT. He made certain guesses which are probably valid. First of all, the story of man is the story of lengthening life expectancy. As man solved problems, both old and new, he extended his life. The men of Sitnalta are quite likely to live 2 or 3 times the span of homoskind or even longer. This is very difficult to judge as time seems to be a creation of man to serve his purpose. I don't think enough time has gone by for man to have conquered death, although that is possible. From earliest times men have known or intuited that immortality was possible to them. They regularly made gods in their images.

In any case, certainly reason is the fountain of youth ascribed to Johnny Eagle at his trial. He described man as a creature of reason who, because reason was man's means of survival, had the longest period of adolescence of any creature of the animal kingdom. Man wasn't born ready to run or hide, nor in a short period could he fight or kill or fly. His continuation depended on development of his mind, which was a cumulative, a hierarchical process; thus, man had the most prolonged childhood and adolescence. At one time in man's history, he reduced the age of majority from 21 to 18 when it would have been healthier to have upped it to 31. Who knows, the age of majority on Sitnalta could be 31 or 51 or 101, said the littlest turtle.

You can be sure, said LGT, that a love of learning is the key to both quantity and quality of manness. If the young of the species learned or were taught to like school, to like problems, they would confront life later on in their majority, she continued, whether that was 31, 51 or 101 as problem-solvers, for that is the meaning of being adult. The adult time of life is the time to do. We don't know how advanced life of Sitnalta might be, but we do know that the adult population will unequivocally do. They will accomplish and not apologize for it. On the existential level, a high standard of living will be common to all. On the theoretical level, the rate of obsolescence will be fantastic.

And everybody will applaud each new advance, interjected LT; then he thought, No, maybe not. Maybe it will just be a way of life. Or maybe the way of life will be to applaud. Certainly every man shall continue to learn even as an adult. If you want to know when you begin to die, he said, don't put any year on it; it's when you stop learning.

They would be a race of giants, he continued, not physically perhaps, but in terms of accomplishments such as seem to have existed only three times previously: The Golden Age of Greece; The Renaissance; and The Age of Reason/Industrial Revolution. Reason, with its consequences, has been the salient characteristic of each of these periods. Those have been times when the advanced and the average levels of rationality among men were significantly different from what went before. Rationality or its absence is the hallmark of a culture.

Just as rationality is the hallmark of a culture, so is it of a man, continued the littlest turtle.

Just a minute before you talk about the individual. What happened to the cultures to cause them to fall? asked the old turtle.

LT smiled because he had just discovered the rudimentary answer, though he didn't know the particulars. And as he explained, he didn't seek to know them; not now, at any rate, when there was too much positive to discover. He explained that the fall of the cultures of reason were a consequence of inroads on reason, whether anti-reason, or non-reason, and that the most important thing to grasp was that this happened not to society but to individuals, albeit on a society-wide basis.

There is no societal mind, no societal stomach, only individual minds and stomachs. The operative effects of the mass of individuals can be called its culture, but it is misleading and destructive to consider mass culture as though there were a collective sense or will or mind or anything else. So you see, he said, one cannot explain what they called the Dark or the Middle Ages without reference to the individuals who lived then. Individually, they seemed to be made up of the non-mind creatures called barbarians and the anti-mind creatures called mystics.

If you don't object, he went on, I would rather not dwell on such creatures because it is painful to contemplate and not particularly productive to do so for to do so is to study the corrupt, the rotting, the destructive side of man. In short, it is man as a sick, ill creature. The illness was of the mind, though the physical side necessarily followed. There was a lowering of life expectancy, famine, running sores, pestilence and all that goes with periods of unreason. Man was mentally ill on a cultural level if you wish, but first and last on an individual basis. To understand this, it is important to turn the telescope around and look through the little end. Instead of examining man the sick creature, examine man at large, man as man, in terms of essentials, not particulars. It pays to determine not a catalogue of symptoms of illness, but a catalogue of the characteristics of health. Man in the past seems to have spent great time on mental illness without ever understanding what mental health was.

It seems they were much given to counting noses. They would establish a norm and if individuals didn't fall within the norm they were deviants of some sort. One would guess, he added, that in a sick society the people who couldn't adjust or reconcile the irreconcilable were potentially the most healthy and most interesting people.

It is of vastly greater importance, then, to understand what mental health is. Mental health, like physical health, is the organism functioning normally in a manner consistent with its nature. In the case of mental health, it is the mind functioning. It is to be alert— alive and aware. It is a process of constant movement, constant change. For a period, the concept "mind" almost disappeared. The scholars said mind was an old fashioned concept. They dissected the brain and examined its parts but could find no mind. There was only a body and a brain.

Strangely, one of the most persevering concepts of our ancestors was the thing people intuited from the word soul. The anti-reason people, whether mystics or neo-mystics, dealt with these related concepts—mind and soul—by negating one and stealing the other. Their soul became the supranatural; that is, it was above or beyond nature—unreal. The mind, they said, didn't exist; it was unreal.

The fact, said LGT, is that both were real; the mind is to the brain as the soul is to the human body. To grasp that, turn to reason, not away from it, for answers. They dissected the brain and found no mind; the body and found no soul. It was after all, they said, only matter.

Only matter, indeed, snorted LT. That is something, not nothing. After they killed man either factually or symbolically, they declared the remainder inanimate. Somehow they failed to make any connection between life and man and matter.

It seems, he resumed, that man had discovered all matter was constructed of atoms. They were tiny things that had a nucleus with electrons circling constantly around. There may have been subatomic particles that existed in the nucleus; maybe there were worlds within that still we don't know, but it is enough to understand that existence on the basic and atomic level is made up of motion and energy as well as a substance. To be is to be moving; constantly moving, he added.

To call matter inanimate is valid, but only in the context called life. In more basic terms matter is full not of life but of movement, LGT joined in. All of existence is put together with atoms, she said, and movement is an essential basic characteristic. In some simple structures of existence, recognition of this allowed the rational to heat and cool their habitats and ten thousand other things. When the structures of existence became more complex, this fundamental of movement was lost to sight. Man was composed of matter, but in a complex way; as a matter of fact, in the most complex way. He could not have *been* but for his complexity. He was more complex than the rest of the animals, and the rest of extants. The thing that distinguished him was his mind. He was the thinking animal. Man was the most complex, the most logical, the most complete extension of existence, of matter, and of movement or energy that had ever been. And yet this fundamental characteristic of not only his nature, but all nature, was not recognized.

They attempted to assign all sorts of beliefs to account for his special position except the logical and necessary extension of basic existence. Man is, was, and will be the logical, non-contradictory (but perhaps not ultimate) extension of existence. In substance and method man was consistent with nature. Not only in body, which he shared with animals, but in mind, which was his distinguishing characteristic.

In the body, movement or energy was called life. It was no accident that man was described as quick or dead. Mentally the same inherent movement (even when at rest) was never recognized. When matter was organized in different ways, science learned to categorize it first broadly, then narrowly, by genus and differentia; in the case of man: he was an animal, genus —homo, that reasoned, differentia—sapiens. No scientist would dream of denying the further properties of earth, air, fire or water, but most balked at defining the further distinguishing properties of man. Those who did did so in terms of non-essentials: man walked erect, had an opposing thumb, employed speech, and was tool using.

It passes all our understanding, said LGT, how they couldn't grasp that the mind was the quick brain just as life was the quick body. The brain is part of the body. A monkey—which walks erect, has an opposing thumb, rudiments of speech, and uses tools—is still an animal. It isn't sapient. To possess a sapient brain is to be one of those creatures which, when considered as a whole—both mind and body—has a soul, for the soul does not exist without the sapient mind.

The mind as the logical and necessary extension of existence, of nature, copies the atom in being constantly in a state of movement. It is impossible to describe the nature of the mind without using an active verb. Man identifies—that is the process; the word that names it is identification. He reasons; but, he is said to possess rationality. He recognizes; that is recognition. The processes of the mind are alive and active; that is the nature of the mind—that is the ultimate nature of nature.

When atomic nature is combined one way it is one thing; when combined another way it is another thing. No miracle. When the atom hydrogen is uncombined it is a light gas. In a certain combination with oxygen it is water. No miracle. When hydrogen is combined in a particular and complex way with oxygen, carbon and nitrogen plus a small amount of phosphorus it is DNA, transmitter of the characteristics of life. No miracle. Some combinations and arrangements are micro-organisms; some are plants; some are animals (one, the most complex, is man). No miracle. That animals are reproductive is no miracle; that's how their arrangements occurred. That they reproduce their own species is no miracle. It would be a miracle if it were otherwise, even in the inanimate, as if an apple tree gave pear fruit. It is no miracle that creatures possessing reason would become the inheritors of the earth, for they are nature's logical extension. One is tempted to say ultimate, but who knows what may happen next. What you may say for sure is that if there is any extension it will be pro life; pro mind; pro soul. Because of this we can't say that the inhabitants of Sitnalta are human but, although we have lost track of comparative time, it is unlikely that they are otherwise.

As a matter of fact, interrupted LT, Johnny Eagle had an interesting point in this regard. It seems that man, or at least marginal man, once had a concept called future shock. Essentially it suggested that man couldn't cope with change. (Validly stated it was that animals, the non-rational, couldn't cope with change.) Accordingly marginal man sought to stop change, to bring things to a standstill. It became an attack on growth and the remedy was thought to be the opposite of growth. What happened, Johnny observed, was that marginal man found decay moved just as fast as growth, if not faster. Things went to pieces with bewildering and inexorable rapidity.

Why did they ever believe, Johnny wondered, that "exponential" didn't apply to decay as well as growth. As things went to hell in a handbasket the proponents of limits and the sufferers of limits were heard to utter over and over again to themselves and to anybody who would listen, "But we never intended this." Johnny labeled that phenomenon past shock. It was succeeded by the lamentation, "Won't anybody listen?"

Johnny has been quoted as saying that when you get what you deserve, that's justice, LGT resumed. To know what you or what man deserves, one must understand the nature of man. Therefore, before one can know what justice is, one must know what man is. But to know what man is is a very complex thing. One must know his nature, which requires knowledge of the primary or fundamental nature of nature. Fundamentally, nature is that which is: existence exists.

That is the building block of the least and the most complex of organisms or relationships. Understanding man's identity is predicated upon identification of that primary. "Existence exists" is Archimedes' fulcrum, Johnny has said. With the lever of reason, man could move the world. All he had to do was find a place to put it. Reality is metaphorically that place.

Once he began to understand who and what he was, he could begin to act. It is justice, said Johnny, that when man understood, he took giant strides; he was a giant. When man let the anti-reason cliques persuade him he was a pygmy, that man was base and depraved, he also got justice.

Johnny established early, apparently, continued LGT, that it was necessary to understand LIFE; and next, life as man, or REASON; after that man could apply reason to life and reap, for good or ill, the inexorable consequences: JUSTICE.

Yes, said the old turtle, I recognize that, that sounds very like the Johnny Eagle of my story, but what of the last two essentials, freedom and happiness?

Think for a minute, said LT. Justice is something that has to do with man's relation to reality, not just what courts, however constituted, say. Courts are instituted so that reasonable men with reasonable differences can reasonably resolve them. If every man were to live alone, there would be no need for courts, but as you yourself told us, LT reminded the old turtle, Johnny at his trial explained that strong, self-reliant individuals can accomplish more in terms of creativity or enjoyment by association with other individuals.

Which brings us, said LGT, to government, which is the means by which individuals organize their associations or relationships or society. The proper function of government in a rational society, of men presumably, is to protect the citizens against the irrationality of others, for every citizen must individually bear the consequences of irrationality against himself. Courts can handle the adjustment of irrational relationships whether by mistake, intent or inadvertence (civil) or malicious intent (criminal). A government is properly constituted to include a police force to deal with domestic irrationals and an army to deal with foreign irrationals. These are virtually the sole legitimate functions of government.

Unfortunately, the majority of mankind's history seems to have been of massive government, government that existed in derogation of reason rather than in support of it. Would it surprise you, Old Turtle, to learn that massive government coincides with man's most irrational times?

No, it wouldn't, said the old turtle. As Johnny Eagle might say, they got their due—that's justice.

LGT clapped in delight and said, And can you finish this, "The government which governs best. . . ."

"Governs least," said the old turtle, amused at her enthusiasm and pleased with his own obviously intelligent response.

Now, said LT, man is such a complex creature that only through complex concepts such as society and government can we get at the issue of freedom.

FREEDOM is a consequence of rationality, while justice belongs to both the rational and the irrational. Justice is broad and deals with man to himself, to the natural world, and to other individuals; but freedom is a much more narrow concept. Mind you, it is fundamental and basic, a natural right, you might say, but it is narrow in that it pertains only to man in organized societies, to governments.

The machinery of justice in an organized society is the construct, the artificial entity called government. When it is rationally organized and run, man experiences freedom; when it is not, he suffers loss of freedom. The only reason that an artificial entity can abuse man's existence is because he ceded it the power to do so in order to have a government. In rational times, this is a government of laws. A government is not a natural entity; it has no rights not contractually given it by men assembled, and it continues at their sufferance.

Unfortunately, or perhaps justly, governments reflect the dominant rationality of a culture. When men become irrational, their governments become abusive. Man justly loses his freedom and perhaps a little bit of his manhood. There are no magic words, no shibboleths that will forever perpetuate liberty, even if once correctly identified and established.

Consider the so-called "Golden Rule:" Do unto others as you would have them do unto you. That statement is neither moral nor immoral; it is amoral. To know the morality of anyone mouthing that, I would have to know whether he were rational or irrational.

185

So it is with a government of laws. Those are not magic words. The laws of irrational men will effect injustice and loss of freedom. In such a society, the more laws the less freedom. That's justice—it is the due of irrational men.

Indeed, said LT, the same words in the hands of irrational men don't mean the same things as in the hands of the rational. There once was a great constitution of a great nation that came to have different meanings in direct relation to the deterioration of rationality in that society. Because of this we may speculate on the probable constitution of Sitnalta. It will be made of five words and only their order is important.

Why only five words? asked the Old Turtle.

Because 50, 500, or 5,000 in the hands of irrational men are only an opportunity for mischief. With only 5 words man will be starkly reminded that liberty, like learning, is an intensely personal thing to be achieved individually. Nobody else can do it for you. If you want it—and a rational man will, you must make it yours—and a rational man will. This is not a burden but a glory of citizenship. No man should be a citizen of an organized society if he can't understand and explain to his children what the moral or intellectual basis of that society is.

The citizens of Sitnalta would be able to understand and explain in a simple way the nature and meaning of the five words. If people (I am reluctant to call them men) couldn't, conceivably they could still inhabit Sitnalta under a suitable contract, but they wouldn't be entrusted with responsibilies of government until they exercised the minimum responsibilities of citizenship.

Once before a great nation in its progressive irrationality gave to all of its inhabitants, in the name of equality, the right and responsibility of government. It was another manifestation of their propensity to nose count. They had the magic word "Democracy" which, like the "Golden Rule," was neither moral nor immoral but amoral. Unfortunately, the words universal suffrage didn't turn out to be magic either and led to universal suffering. Their pleas that they didn't intend the consequences, wouldn't anybody listen, were answered only by the irrational who fed irrationality by saying, We will listen—we have answers or programs or policies or laws. The last thing the practitioners of universal suffrage wanted to hear was that this is a just world, inexorably just.

What are the five words? asked the Old Turtle.

Can you guess? replied the LGT.

Life, Reason, Justice, Freedom. . . . the Old Turtle paused.

And the last, said LGT.

Was it Johnny Eagle's last word—HAPPINESS? whispered the Old Turtle.

Yes, Happiness, she responded. Life, Reason, Justice, Freedom and Happiness.

Why Happiness and why is the order important? asked the Old Turtle.

Because, answered the LT, all knowledge is hierarchical. Concepts are based on concepts; they get more and more complex as they reach away from the real world's referents. Man must first understand that exis-

tence exists. That is the fundamental real world refer-
ent. He is, but he is of a certain nature, i.e., possessing reason. That is infinitely more complex. Next he
must apply his existence possessing reason to life as he
encounters it. That results in justice. Then he must
maximize his experiences as best he is able. That results in freedom and then. . . .

And then. . . , repeated the Old Turtle.

And then . . . he gets happiness, the necessary and
inexorable consequence of life, reason, justice, and
freedom. Happiness is man's reward for his effort, the
effect he has caused.

The Old Turtle thought for a long time. Finally he
said, But people have experienced happiness before in
their lives.

Yes, gently rejoined LGT, and such happiness was
always and inevitably the consequence of some
achievement in their lives, however great or small. It
really isn't hard to reach and there is no end to it. It is
the natural high in man's life.

As a society, once, man almost put it all together.
He described man as having certain inalienable rights,
among them life, liberty and the pursuit of happiness . . . but, he perceived those rights through an
overlay of irrationality. Until he was prepared to add
reason and justice, he would get only close and would
necessarily lose even that which he had achieved.

The Old Turtle paid many subsequent visits to LT and LGT. His aging seemed to have been arrested. He was paid particular esteem among those of his acquaintance. They would ask him the secret of his longevity, but to his constant disappointment they never seemed to listen. Never mind, thought the Old Turtle, I still have my visits with LT and LGT. During one of the last of these the Old Turtle remembered that all this had started as a search for Johnny Eagle.

I still haven't given up the search for Johnny Eagle, said LT. It's just that:

a) I think the way to find Sitnalta is by thinking.

b) Maybe Johnny Eagle will find me.

c) Maybe there never was the Johnny Eagle of legend; maybe I am Johnny Eagle.

The Old Turtle smiled and said, Maybe you are. You have lived alone, partly by choice, and partly otherwise. You have no idea how you have gradually changed in these years. You look like a young god. If you would like to know what you look like, come with me to the last remaining artifact, the statue of Johnny Eagle.

After seeing the statue, LT was much moved. Do I look like that?

Yes, breathed LGT.

As do you, he responded . . . with a difference. He paused. A very important difference, though he didn't pause to figure out why he said so.

That was one of their last meetings. It was no surprise to the Old Turtle that the day came when he no longer could find LT or LGT. All he was to find was a paper with words. It said:

> Dearest Turtle Teacher:
> We know you can understand that the journey on which we are about to set out is not for you as well.
> We hope that you will find happiness in the happiness you have helped us find. No matter how exciting our future searches may be, surely none shall match the first—the search for reason which we have shared with you.
> We have made characters similar to the books for this message and hope you can translate it.
> With the measure of love possible only to MAN we wish you
>   Love—Man and Woman

Later the Old Turtle was found dead at his home with that paper in his grip. The barber surgeon told turtle's relatives that as near as he could determine the Old Turtle's heart had burst, but, he added, it must have been painless because he died with a smile.

What, of course, none of them understood was that though the Old Turtle was very set in his ways, he still was a being of considerable soul.

EPILOGUE

The rumor persists even to this day that there was a Johnny Eagle and a new world of Sitnalta.

It is said that Johnny and Quen and their associates lived happily ever after. . . .

(. . . or at least for so long as they worked very hard at it —
J. E.)

LIST OF ILLUSTRATIONS
WITH CREDITS

The author and editor thank those individuals and institutions to whom credit is given below for their assistance in supplying the original illustration material. Philosophical or editorial application is the sole responsibility of the author or editor.

Chapter I   IN THE BEGINNING

12/13 *A Most Peculiar Place* San Francisco, with the Marin County hills in the background. Photograph by ROBERT CAMERON, 1978.

14 *The State Institute of Science and Planning* A composite drawing executed by PAUL BENEMELIS, 1978.

16 *Early Homos* AUGUSTE RODIN, *ADAM*, 1881, bronze. *EVE, AFTER THE FALL*, 1886, Marble. Courtesy of the Art Institute of Chicago.

18 *Homo Family Celebrating the Declaration of Instinct* STATUES FROM THE TEMPLE OF ABU, Tell Asmar, circa 2750 B.C., marble. Oriental Institute, University of Chicago.

20 *Other Early Transitional Creatures* From upper left to lower right

GILIAK PROTECTIVE HOUSE SPIRIT, Eastern Siberia, wood. National Museum of Denmark, Copenhagen.

JOMON FIGURINE, Japan, 2nd-1st millennium B.C., clay. Collection des Musees Nationaux, Musee Guimet, Paris.

JACQUES LIPCHITZ, *FIGURE*, 1926–1930, bronze. Hirshhorn Museum and Sculpture Garden, Smithsonian Institution, Washington, D.C.

COLOMBIAN FIGURINE, Quimbaya style, District of Caldas, clay with gold nose ring. Etnografiska Museum, Goteborg.

195

Chapter II JOHNNY EAGLE: THE FLEDGLING

31 *. . . Ultimately Yielded the More Efficient Homo Animal*

Clockwise from upper right

GLEGLE AS A LION
BEHANZIN AS A SHARK
Both, Abomey, Dahomey, clay and polychrome. Collection Musee de l'Homme, Paris.

The Kingdom of Abomey, led by Glegle (1858–1899) and his contemporary, Behanzin, flourished through its slave-trade economy. It was annexed by French troops in 1894.

TLACUACHE, part weasel, part man, Azpotec, Monte Alban IV, 800–1200 A.D., ceramic. Museo Regional de Antropologia, Oaxaca.

Monte Alban was a city dedicated entirely to the glory of the gods. The Zapotec designers, artisans, and even laborers are said to have been intent on close communion with their gods. Alternative pictures could be of the flaying god who wore the victim's skin or the bat vampire goddess. Monte Alban is one of the most impressive ruins in Mexico today.

SIMHAVAKTRA DAKINI, Lamaist, 18th century A.D., lacquered wood. The lion-faced dakini (feminine divinity of lesser rank) once danced upon a human figure, now lost. Her right hand once held a chopper and her left a skull bowl. Asian Art Museum of San Francisco, The Avery Brundage Collection. Description by the museum.

34 *A Plethora of Transitional Snoxes*
An Egyptian pantheon, clockwise from upper right, then center

THOTH, advocate of Osiris, possessor of ingenuity and invention, gave names to things, invented letters, instituted worship, arithmetic, music, and sculpture.

ASAR-HAPI (SERAPIS), god of the underworld, lord of eternity, prince of everlastingness.

RENNUT, goddess of the harvest, one of the many attributes of Isis who possessed great skill in the working of magic.

SET, god of the night sky, personification of darkness, night, chaos, death and evil, referred to as Typhon by Plutarch.

ISIS, goddess of words of power, in cow-headed form, created new beings and restored the dead. It is impossible to limit the attributes of Isis, her priests having united in her one or more of the attributes of all the goddesses of Egypt known to us. Her worship spread to several places in Western Europe.

SEBEK-RA, prince of the powers of darkness. Plutarch explained the crocodile's supposed absence of a tongue with "divine reason needeth not speech."

KHENSU-NEFER-HETEP, early predynastic lord of gods, probable moon good when worship of the moon preceded the sun, later possessor of absolute power over evil spirits which infested earth, air, sea, and sky and brought to man pain, sickness, disease, decay, madness and death.

36 *Homohetero . . .*

GENIUS, holding symbols of fertility, power and royalty, after an Assyrian relief from the Palace of Ashurnasirpal II (883–859 B.C.). Original located at New York Metropolitan Museum of Art.

EAGLE-HEADED GENIUS, after an Assyrian relief from the Northwest Palace of Ashurnasirpal II at Nimrud. Original located at the Louvre, Paris.

TIAMAT (or CHAOS), after an Assyrian relief from Nimrud, 9th century B.C. Original located at The British Museum, London.

37 *. . . Genesis*

LION-MAN, after an Assyrian relief from the Palace of Sennacherib (705–681 B.C.) at Ninevah. Original located at The British Museum, London.

SPHINX, after a Neo-Hittite relief from Carchemish, 1050–850 B.C. Original located at the Archaeological Museum, Ankara.

LION-GRIFFIN, after an Achaemenid glazed brick relief from Susa, 5th century B.C. Original located at the Louvre, Paris.

Drawings, pages 34, 36 and 37 by JUDITH SUTTON, 1978.

40 *Mother Superior, Natal Early Start Training Centers*

LEONINE FIGURINE, Mesopotamian, Proto-Elamite, circa 3,500–3,000 B.C., crystalline limestone. The Brooklyn Museum, lent by Mr. Robin B. Martin.

Sometimes titled The Mother Goddess or Monster, the mythical beast has been said by Henri Frankfort to convincingly express the terror with which man realizes his helplessness in a hostile universe.

42/43 *Ordinary Nest Homo*
SHE-WOLF WITH ROMULUS AND REMUS, Etruscan, 500 B.C. (twins added in the 16th century), bronze. Capitolino Museo, Rome.

45 *Eagle Tribe Development*
Upper left to lower right

Wild (Free): an American bald eagle, perched on a mountain ledge with his wings inverted, right talon thrust forward on a pine sapling. After reverse, Walking Liberty half dollar, 1916–1947, United States of America.

Drawing by CELESTE ERICSSON, 1978.

Heraldic Devices: *Early,* Greek; *Upstart,* Napoleon Bonaparte; *Established,* West Prussian; *Dogmatic,* Pope Alexander IV; *Midevil,* Gothic; *Inheritor,* Roman; *Cadet,* Macedonian.

Drawings by ERNST LEHNER, *Symbols, Signs & Signets* (1950), Dover Pictorial Archive Series, Dover Publications, 1969.

Carrier, suggested by teratornis, eagle-like vulture of the Pleistocene era, an old world affinity vulture found among the diurnal raptorial birds of Rancho la Brea, California.

Drawing by CELESTE ERICSSON, 1978.

Chapter III JOHNNY EAGLE: THE YOUTH

48 *Level One Inmate Visited by Parents*

GILGAMESH GRAPPLING WITH TWO HUMAN-HEADED BULLS, detail, shell inlay on the soundbox of a harp, Ur, third millennium B.C. University Museum, Philadelphia.

50-51 *Some of Society's Re-educators*

Upper left to lower right

CHINESE BUDDHIST DEMON, after a detail from a Chinese Buddhist painting depicting judgment in the seventh hell. Original located at the Horniman Museum, London.

One Buddhist system has eight major hells and sixteen minor hells for different types of wickedness. The self is considered an illusion; personal immortality is considered an obstacle to Nirvana, a sometime definition of which is the abandonment of existence.

AUSTRALIAN TRIBAL SPIRITS, male and female, after a bark painting, unknown artist of Gagadju tribe. Original located at the National Museum, Victoria.

MAGDALENIAN DANCING SORCERER OR TRIBAL MEDICINE MAN, after the Paleolithic cave painting at Trois Freres, Ariege.

JAPANESE BUDDHIST TORMENTER, after a detail from a Japanese Buddhist painting depicting the motif of the weighing of the souls of the dead. Original located at the Horniman Museum, London.

Fiery hells and agonies are prominent sufferings in Eastern and Western mysticism alike as are torments of being flogged, flayed, racked, dismembered, disembowelled, hacked, pierced, torn, impaled, blinded, throttled, suffocated, crushed, hanged by the neck, feet, arms, tongue, ears, genitals, hair, heart, etc. The agonies differ little in particular, the primary difference being that Buddhist and Hindu victims are recycled. All traditional mystics, however, deny man not only independent life but the correlative independent death.

ITALIAN RENAISSANCE CHARON, transporter of the souls of the dead, after a detail from MICHELANGELO's THE LAST JUDGMENT, 1435–1441, fresco. Original located in the Sistine Chapel, Rome.

MIXTEX GOD OF LEARNING AND THE PRIESTHOOD, Quetzalcoatl, after a representation in the Codex Fejervary Mayer. Original located at the City of Liverpool Museums.

DEMON, after a detail from HANS MEMLING's THE LAST JUDGMENT, 1472. Original located at the Pomeranian Museum, Gdansk.

AZTEC LORD OF THE DEAD, Mictlantecuhtli, after a ceramic from Tierra Blanca, Vera Cruz, circa 600–900. Original located at the Museo de Antropologia de la Universidad Veracruzana, Jalapa.

The paintings of primitive man probably sought to evoke control over a mystifying world. The practical hunter practiced the conceptual skill of art to aid understanding of his relation to the world and to celebrate that he was different. The usual religious or magical wish-picture reason advanced for this art does not give proper emphasis to the insight of Cro-Magnon man or of art as a means of understanding. That Cro-Magnon man painted many new heads over earlier pictures reflected insight. That bison did not paint standing man also helped put the world in perspective.

EGYPTIAN HORSE, after a painting from the unlocated tomb of Neb-Amon, Thebes. Original located at The British Museum, London.

MINOAN BULL, after a wall painting, circa 1,500 B.C., in the Palace of Knossos, Crete.

BYZANTINE GOATS, after a floor mosaic, 6th century, at the Great Palace, Constantinople.

MIOCENE PRIMATE, Ramapithecus, thought to be the oldest of Homo sapiens ancestors in a direct line, existing fourteen million years ago.

While modern theory rejects the 19th century concept of a chain of being with its missing link in favor of a more complex network of strands of evolving populations, too much emphasis is still placed on the 19th century concept of "natural selection." As man (or proto-man) was not born by an act of creation, neither was he created secondhandedly, i.e. by force of events or terrain.

Man created himself, first, last, and always, by grasping and understanding (to the extent of his capacity) who and where he was. Such insights account for the periodic epochal advancements of our ancestors. For the periodic retrogression of collateral species not destined to be our ancestors, look to life without understanding (aping) or to life destructive of understanding (religion and mysticism—for which see the Western Neanderthaler).

Drawings by JUDITH SUTTON, 1978.

Chapter IV   THE TRIAL OF JOHNNY EAGLE

78 *We Are Confused*
Suggested by the ancient Egyptian motif of the weighing of souls. As to the prosecutors, in Christian perpetuation of the theme: GIS-LEBERTUS, detail from *THE LAST JUDGMENT,* 12th century, stone, Cathedral of Autun; and, detail from *THE LAST JUDGMENT,* mid-13th century, marble, Cathe-

dral at Bourges. As to the judge: Egyptian studies of Ammet, devourer of souls of the unjustified: *PAPYRUS OF ANHAI,* Nos. 10,470 and 10,472, and the *GREENFIELD PAPYRUS,* No. 10,554; all at The British Museum, London.

Illustration by HEATHER PRESTON, 1978.

Chapter V   THE LABORS OF JOHNNY EAGLE

Chapter VI   IN THE ENDING

Chapter VII   *SITNALTA*

170 *Quen Eagle*
VICTORY OF SAMOTHRACE,
circa 200 B.C., marble. Louvre,
Paris.

190 *Johnny Eagle*
JOSEPH UPHUES (1850–1911),
bronze, detail. Private collection.

Endpapers
JOHANN CHRYSOSTOM WOLFGANG
AMADEUS MOZART (1756–1791),
AH, VOUS DIRAI-JE, MAMAN,
Theme and Variations VI, VIII,
and IX. Based on a theme attrib-
uted to NICOLAS DEZEDE (1740?–
1792).
Rendered by WILLIAM PASKETT,
1978.

Cover Illustration
LEONARDO DA VINCI, *DIAGRAM
OF A RIBBED WING PARTLY
COVERED WITH SILK,* Ms. B, fol.
74 r., detail. Bibliotheque, Institut
de France, Paris.

EDITOR'S NOTES

1. A word about the author. Jason Alexander is the *nom de guerre* of a person engaged in several pursuits, one of which is writing. *Johnny Eagle* is a spin-off or exercise arising from the commencement of a trilogy of romantic novels of applied philosophy.

2. Use of any artist's work herein does not express endorsement of or comment upon any work not included or not consistent philosophically with the included work.

3. Johnny Eagle will subsequently appear in a hardcover edition and in such other forms of publication as are appropriate.

4. The art for the proposed hardcover jacket has not been determined or selected. The author would like an original oil entitled "The Four R's" (Reading, wRiting, aRithmetic, Reason) and invites artists to submit appropriate works for the cover. Prizes will be awarded for the art selected (if any) according to the following categories:

First	$2,500
Second	$1,000
Third	$ 500

Works selected shall become the property of the author. There shall be a jury of one whose decision is final. Subsequent use of the painting(s) shall be at the sole discretion of the author. California-domiciled artists need not apply unless their work qualifies for exception from California Civil Code Section 986.

Any work considered must be submitted pursuant to terms and conditions provided in the submission form which may be procured from the editor, Post Office Box 42422, San Francisco, California 94101.

5. Asked to comment upon the noticeable omission of the art movements of the past half century, the author responded substantially as follows:

> The more recent Pop Art, Op Art, Metaphysical Art, Symbolist Art, Total Art, Neo-Plasticism, Purism, Constructionism, ad-nauseamism have been omitted as they are almost too mindless to satirize, parody, or comment upon.

> In a similar vein, macrame, constructions, collages, montages, stencils, beadwork, tooled leather or other arts and crafts techniques belong to the realm of the decorative arts, itself a valid subject, but this book is too fundamental to analyze or comment upon the supportive values of wallpaper design.

> The so-called People's Art or wall murals belong as much to literature as art since they tell a story not otherwise communicable to or by the non-lettered, functioning more or less as intra-urban primitive ideographs.

> The field of Aesthetics, which includes Art, is the most wide open, exciting challenge facing modern man. It is the last frontier of understanding. Most great art is yet to come. In this, as in all other aspects of life, the future belongs to the rational man.

6. Acknowledgement is given to the many individuals whose courtesy and competence filled blanks in the editor's notebook during the course of the book's progress to production. It is particularly due to several whose professional skills were employed in bringing the book to its final form and whose names do not appear in the Colophon or the List of Illustrations with Credits: Barbara Hack, Joseph Fay, Nagel Parkhurst, and Edwin Hoffman.

COLOPHON

Compositor	TYPESETTING SERVICES OF CALIFORNIA
Typeface	PALATINO
Printer	THE MARIER ENGRAVING COMPANY
Binder	MOUNTAIN STATES BINDERY
Paper	NEKOOSA SUPER OPAQUE
Paper Merchant	BLAKE, MOFFITT & TOWNE A SAXON INDUSTRIES COMPANY
Production Consultant	GREG HUBIT

Var. VIII.
Minore.

Var: IX.
Maggiore.